To Lois + K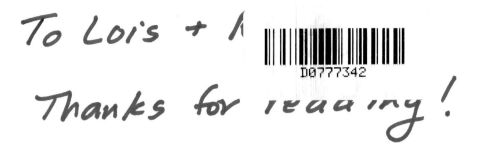

Thanks for reading!

Love,

Margy

Margaret Turner Taylor
July 2020

The Quilt Code

THE QUILT CODE

Margaret Turner Taylor

This book is a work of fiction. Many of the names, places, characters, and incidents are products of the author's imagination or are used fictitiously. Any resemblance to actual events or locales or person living or dead is entirely coincidental.

Copyright © 2020 Llourettia Gates Books, LLC
All rights reserved. This book or any portion thereof may not be reproduced or used in any manner whatsoever without the express written permission of the publisher.

Llourettia Gates Books, LLC
P.O. Box #411
Fruitland, Maryland 21826

www.margaretttaylorwrites.com

Hardcover ISBN: 978-1-7347347-3-7
Paperback ISBN: 978-1-7347347-4-4
eBook ISBN: 978-1-7347347-5-1
Library of Congress Control Number: 2020908988

Cover design by Jaime L. Coston
Photography by Andrea López Burns
Interior design and layout by Jamie Tipton, Open Heart Designs

*This book is dedicated with all my love
to Louisa Ann Sevigny*

Contents

Preface

My granddaughter Louisa, for whom this book is written, did the artwork for the cover when she was in the second grade at Pinehurst Elementary School. Her art teacher selected Louisa's colorful painting to be displayed in an art show at the Wicomico County Public Library. In addition to being the amazing cover of the book, Louisa's work was the inspiration for the story and the title of *The Quilt Code*. Her beautiful design reminded me of a quilt.

When I was young, I helped my grandmother and my great grandmother work on the wonderful quilts they were sewing. I remember that the quilting frame was set up in a spare bedroom and seemed to fill the entire space. I sat on a high stool to be able to see and touch the magical work. The quilters occasionally allowed me to sew a few crooked stitches with my awkward tiny fingers. As an adult, I have designed and made a number of quilts of my own.

Louisa's book was always going to be some kind of a mystery story. Louisa had visited the Harriet Tubman museums in Cambridge, Maryland and in Church Creek, Maryland, and she told me all about her field trips. The museums and learning about Harriet Tubman's life made quite an impression on her. It all came together for us, and Louisa loved the idea that her book would be set in 1860. We chose *The Quilt Code* as the title, and I began to write. Louisa's pre-Civil War alter ego is the main character in the story.

If you look very carefully, you can find the letters of her first name, **L-O-U-I-S-A,** hidden in the design on the cover. I have to give all the credit to my exceptional granddaughter. Her painting was the original cypher, the secret message, the code, out of which the idea for this book was born.

This work of fiction, a story for young people, is about life in 1860 in the border state of Maryland. It is about how the Underground Railroad *might* have worked to move slaves from bondage to freedom and about how one rural family *might* have participated in this effort. *The Quilt Code* hypothesizes how one specific quilt code *might* have been used in a local area and in a dynamic way, to communicate among a small group of people who wanted to help slaves escape. Their code was small-scale and very closely held.

CHAPTER ONE

Summer on the Farm

19-21-13-13-5-18   15-14   20-8-5   6-1-18-13

oday is my last day of school until next fall. I guess I'm excited that summer is here, but the truth is, I love to learn new things. I have fun playing with my school friends. I live on a farm, and for every child who lives on a farm, the summer is not really a vacation. Summer just means there's a different kind of work to do. Even though the work is hard sometimes, I don't mind.

I am Louisa Taylor Gates, and I'm twelve years old. My mother is Abigail Taylor Gates. My father died in a farming accident a few weeks before I was born, so I never knew him. My older brother, Joseph Taylor Gates, is named after our father. Joseph is fourteen. All three of us have to work

1

hard to keep the farm going. We have hired hands who work on the farm, and all of them work hard, too.

We have two hundred acres near the town of Burley, Maryland, and our homestead, Elderberry Farm, is two miles from town. Burley is on the Eastern Shore of Maryland, just a few miles from the Atlantic Ocean. We grow cotton, flax, wheat, corn, oats, timothy, and lots and lots of vegetables. We also have pigs, sheep, chickens, two goats, and two cows. We milk the cows and drink their milk and make butter and cheese. We milk the goats and make soap out of their milk. We make a lot of soap and sell it. Everybody loves our goat milk soap.

It's 1860, and this is a very upsetting political time in Burley, in the state of Maryland, and in the United States of America. Our elders are always talking about the issues of the day, and there are tremendous divisions in their opinions. The main problem right now is slavery, and everybody has a strong view about that. Some people say they have to have slaves to preserve their livelihoods, that slaves are necessary to pick the cotton to keep farms and plantations prosperous. The owners of cotton plantations say that slave labor is the growth engine of the economy in the South. They believe that slavery is a law of God, that owning slaves is a "God-given right." Other people say the federal government has no right to tell the states what to do. Still others say slavery is immoral and must be abolished. Slavery is always a dangerous topic for discussion, and it makes people very angry. The issue of slavery divides families and destroys friendships.

My family is completely on the side of abolishing slavery. My grandmother is Priscilla Emerson Taylor, and we call her Gram. My dear Gram openly calls herself an abolitionist. She believes that slavery is evil. She makes no apologies for her strong views. My mother and my grandfather agree with her. My grandfather is Edward Preston Taylor. We call him Grandpa Doc. My mother and Grandpa Doc might not be as outspoken as Gram, but they feel just as passionately about not owning slaves. We have dark-skinned people who work for us. We call them Negroes. They live and work on our farm, but they are free people. We pay them wages for their work and give them houses. But they are free to leave, to walk away from our farm, at any time. We don't own them. We believe it is morally wrong to own another human being.

Some people who live on neighboring farms and plantations own their workers. These workers are their slaves. They don't get paid wages, and they are not free to leave their owners. Slave owners say they have invested their money in slaves and that legally, slaves are their economic assets. They believe that slaves have no right to try to escape their bondage. Our family has bought some of these slaves and given them their freedom. Several of our neighbors don't like our family very much because we speak out and because we have given Negroes their freedom. I am a strong abolitionist myself, but I don't say too much in school about what I think. Some of my friends are from families who own many slaves.

During the school year, I ride my pony to school in Burley every day, rain or shine. I'm lucky to have a pony to ride. My brother Joseph also has a pony to ride to school. Some of my friends who live on farms, even farther away from town than Elderberry Farm, have to walk to and from school every day. Joseph and I leave our ponies at our grandparents' house during the school day. They have a barn for horses, and they live right across the street from the Burley School. Every day after school, before we ride our ponies home to the farm, my brother and I go to our grandparents' house for milk and cookies.

Our grandfather is a doctor, so he and Gram have to live in town. He has his doctor's office in one part of the big house where they live. He's the only doctor for miles around, and he takes care of everybody in town and everybody in most of Worcester County. He makes house calls, even in the middle of the night and even in the middle of a snow storm.

My grandparents come out to visit us on the farm all the time, and we go to their house every Sunday for a big dinner after church. My grandmother is a good cook, and she also has a very good cook who works for her. Her cook, Celia, is a paid worker, as my grandmother is always pointing out. They do not own her, and she is free to leave my grandparents' home at any time. My grandparents won't have anyone working for them who isn't free. They feel strongly about this. They hire other Negroes to work in their gardens and in the house. All their workers are free men and women, and they get paid for the work they do. Sometimes people get tired of hearing my grandmother say that all of the people who work for her and my grandfather are free and receive wages. That kind of talk makes slave owners angry.

This summer I will spend many hours working in my mother's gardens. She has four gardens, and I work in all of them. My mother works hard in all of her gardens, too. She has a kitchen garden that's on one side of our back door where she grows lettuce and tomatoes and other things that go in salads. On the other side of the back door is her herb garden. My mother grows all kinds of herbs. I think she loves her herb garden the best, and sometimes she just stands beside that garden and looks at the neat rows of chives, parsley, thyme, and lavender. She also grows mint, rosemary, and other kinds of medicinal herbs. She has a large flower garden at the side of the house where she has both perennials and annuals. It's a lot of work to keep the weeds out of that garden. Weeds seem to really love the flower garden.

Then there is the biggest garden of all that isn't close to the house. That's where we grow the vegetables that we sell. We also dry and preserve these vegetables, and we put them up in glass jars to eat during the winter. These are the vegetables that require more space to grow. This garden has to be plowed between the rows, and large crops grow there, like sweet corn, white potatoes, yams, cabbages, onions, squash, melons, and pumpkins. Most of the time, one of our hired hands plows and weeds this big garden. We help pick the vegetables.

We also have a fruit orchard, but I don't really count that as a garden. It is even farther from the house, and our hired hands tend the orchard. My mother uses all the fruit that is harvested from the trees. We gather apples, pears, apricots, figs, and plums. We are fortunate to have good soil on our farm, and we are lucky we have hard-working hands to help us take care of it.

We pay the Negroes who work for us a good wage, and we give them all a place to live. Some of them work in the farm fields, and some of them help my mother in the house. My mother makes sure everyone who lives and works on our farm has enough to eat and presentable clothes to wear. My mother and Grandpa Doc help to deliver our workers' babies when they are born, and we are always there to take care of them when they are sick. We like our hired hands and take good care of them, and they like working for us. My mother and brother and I could never keep the farm going without them. It takes all of us working hard all the time to make a living on a farm.

But we don't work *all* the time. We have fun times, too. After church and after the chores are done, everybody takes the day off on Sunday. The Negroes who work at Elderberry Farm don't work on Sunday either. My mother, my brother, and I spend most of our Sundays in town with Gram and Grandpa Doc. Sometimes during the summer we go on picnics after church.

Whenever I don't have chores in the house or chores in the gardens, I sneak off and read my books, no matter what day it is. My books are precious to me, and I take good care of them. There's a spot not far from the house where I can sit under the trees and read. It is my secret hiding place, and no one bothers me there. It's cool there in the summer, and I love having my own special retreat.

I have a little dog named Cranky. She's not really cranky at all and has a happy and cheerful disposition. I don't know why she got the name Cranky. She's a fluffy, all-white dog, a mix of poodle and some kind of miniature terrier. She's quite small, but she has lots of spirit and is exceptionally smart. I love her to pieces, and she always comes and sleeps beside me when I go to my special reading hideout in the woods. She sleeps in my room every night.

My brother is two years older than I am, and in September, he's going all the way to Washington, D.C. to live with my aunt and uncle and our cousins, Lane and Richard. There is an excellent private school in Washington, and my grandparents and my mother want my brother to go to that school so he can get an outstanding education. It costs money to attend the Quaker day school, and my grandparents are going to pay for him to attend. It is our good fortune to have family in the District of Columbia, so he can live with them while he goes to school. This summer will be our last few months together before he goes off to stay in Washington, D.C. for the school year.

Joseph will be spending the summer at my grandparents' house. They've hired a tutor who will teach him the things he needs to know before he can go away to school in the fall. He's smart, but we all want to be sure he's not behind when he begins his lessons in September. He's not happy about being told he has to study or about being cooped up inside all summer. I will miss him when he goes away to school.

My family doesn't think I know they are part of what they call the Underground Railroad. Since I was eight years old, I've known that my grandparents and my mother help slaves escape to freedom. Once when I was spending the night at my grandparents' house in town, I overheard a conversation. A slave who was trying to escape from his plantation in Virginia had come to their house in the middle of the night. Gram and Grandpa Doc had not been expecting anybody, and they were talking about what to do with him. They thought I was asleep. But I listened to everything they had to say, and I figured it out.

They don't think I know what they are doing. They think I'm too young to understand, and they probably think I can't keep a secret. I know it has to be a secret, and I have kept their secret all these years. My mother also helps move slaves to freedom in many ways. She puts quilts on the clothesline outside our back door, and each of these special quilts sends a specific message. She does a good job of hiding what she does from me, but I know what is going on. I hope she will soon realize I'm old enough to tell me about what they are up to and let me help. I know my family is trying to protect me by keeping their activities hidden from me. But I am now grown up enough, and I can help. If they don't tell me what they are doing by this summer, I'm going to tell them I know all about it and want to participate.

A big national election is coming up this fall. A man named Abraham Lincoln is running to be elected President of the United States. My family is a big supporter of Mr. Lincoln. My mother and my grandparents believe that Mr. Lincoln is the only candidate for President who has the courage to end slavery. Some people say that if Lincoln is elected, the slave states will secede from the Union. These southern states want slavery to continue to be legal, and they may try to form their own country so they can continue to own slaves. Maryland is a border state, located between the slave states and the free states, caught right in the middle of the slavery mess. We fear the states in the South will secede from the rest of the country and that the United States is headed for a civil war. It's a big problem right now, and everyone in my family is very worried about it.

CHAPTER TWO

A Stormy Night

1   19-20-15-18-13-25   14-9-7-8-20

e'd gone to a church picnic that Sunday afternoon, and the drive on the bumpy dirt road to the Sinepuxent Bay beach seemed to take forever. Gram and Grandpa Doc drove us all to the picnic in their big wagon. Celia made her famous fried chicken to take in our basket, and we had many good things to eat. I love potato salad, and some of the ladies from our church brought big bowls of it to the picnic. Everybody wanted a slice of Celia's triple chocolate cake, and it almost disappeared before I got a piece.

Joseph and I and the other children liked to play on Assateague Island, a barrier island that is a strip of sand

and a wild and favorite place to explore. Assateague is quite close to the mainland at this point, and small row boats carried us the short distance, back and forth across the Sinepuxent Bay, the small body of water between the island and the mainland We went swimming in the tidal pools along the beach and dug holes and built structures in the sand. I love being beside the ocean and watching the waves come in and go out. We had relay races, and played tag and hide-and-seek in the woods near the water.

We couldn't take any food with us when we went to play on Assateague Island. Wild ponies live on the island. Most of the time they are shy and hide in the woods. But if they smell food, they overcome their shy ways and stampede out of the woods to try to find the food. Then there will be trouble. They like to chase us to get the food, and the ponies will bite. They bite hard, and it hurts like the dickens. I have never been bitten, but I've seen other people get too close to the hungry ponies. The ponies are small and look nice and friendly, but I have learned that it's best to leave them alone.

It was hot and sunny that Sunday afternoon. Because my skin is fair, my mother insists that I wear a hat when I'm outside, playing in the sun. I wore my sunbonnet, but I got a sunburn on my face anyway. It was a long day, and the fun lasted into the evening. We had to be sure that everyone was safely back across the Sinepuxent Bay before the sun went down. When it grew dark, we sang hymns around a huge campfire on the mainland.

My brother and I were tired, and it was way past our bedtime. My mother was tired, too. We climbed into the wagon to drive back to Burley from Assateague Island, and I was asleep against Mama's shoulder as soon as the wagon began to roll.

Because it was late and everybody was so tired, my mother decided we should sleep at my grandparents' house in town rather than get on our horses and ride the rest of the way home to Elderberry Farm. Gram and Grandpa Doc have plenty of bedrooms in their house, so they carried Joseph and me upstairs to bed and didn't even wake us up.

Loud voices woke me in the middle of the night. I peeked out the door of my bedroom and could see Gram standing in the downstairs hallway in her dressing gown and wearing the white cotton cap she uses to cover her white hair when she sleeps. She likes to keep her hair clean and white, without any dust in it, so at night she wraps her braid around her head and puts on a sleeping cap. She says she gets dust in her hair during the night, and the dust makes her sneeze. Tonight, her braid had come loose and hung down her back, but she still had on her cap. So that I could better see and hear what was going on, I crept closer to the railing that overlooked the downstairs hall. Nobody could see me.

"We thought you were coming last night. My daughter and her two children are asleep upstairs. Please, be as quiet as you can be. Come in through the back, and we will go right to the cellar. I'll be down there in a minute." Not all the houses on the Eastern Shore of the Chesapeake Bay have basements as big as the one in my grandparents' house. Lots of people have root cellars. They're called root cellars because people store their root vegetables there to preserve them during the winter months. Root vegetables are potatoes, carrots, onions, beets, turnips, parsnips, and any other vegetable that you have to dig out of the ground. Root cellars are tiny and cramped and smell bad. They are also good for hiding from hurricanes, northeastern storms, and tornadoes.

Because we are living on a sandbar on the Eastern Shore, when you dig down into the ground, it isn't long before you hit water. In the town of Burley, many of the larger houses do have basements. These are really just big cellars and have dirt floors. They all smell musty. Nobody wants to spend much time down there. But my grandparents' basement is special.

They don't know that I know about the secret opening that's behind the big wooden hutch they keep in their cellar. My brother and I discovered it one day a year or so ago. If you open the lower doors in the hutch and push on one of the wooden panels at the rear, that panel falls backwards through a hole in the wall. This hole in the wall is really the entrance to a tunnel. Joseph and I climbed into the hutch, through its back, and through the hole in the wall. We followed the long tunnel all the way to its end. The tunnel's exit is at the side of a short rise in the land. This small hill is in the woods, close to a creek bed. The opening from the tunnel is hidden very well. You would never know it was there, if you hadn't crawled through the tunnel and come out beside Crooked Creek.

When there is a lot of rain and the creek overflows its banks, water gets into the tunnel. That happens mostly during the early spring. It is late May now, and the creek is not usually full in May. Parts of the creek bed are dry for much of the summer, except when there is a bad thunder storm and a torrential downpour.

When I heard my Gram talking about the cellar, I knew there must be someone in the house who was being moved along the Underground Railroad. They had turned up unexpectedly at Gram and Grandpa Doc's door. I think that might happen often at their house. Running something that has to be kept secret is always dangerous and always unpredictable. You have to be able to expect the unexpected and to adapt quickly to changing conditions and circumstances. Tonight was one of those nights.

After we'd all gone to bed, there had been a loud thunderstorm with lots of thunder and lightning. It was raining hard when I woke up to the sound of voices in the hall below. The storm must be what the discussion was about. Because of the hard rain, something about this slave's escape plan had gone wrong and had to be changed.

Gram was expressing concern about flooding in the tunnel. Grandpa Doc was holding a lighted lantern, ready to go down to the cellar. I couldn't see who was with them, but I did hear more than one strange voice. Then I heard a baby cry. I knew there were usually no babies in Gram's house, so the crying baby must belong to one of the slaves who was trying to get to freedom. I knew I should go back to bed and leave this to my mother and my grandparents, but when I heard the baby crying, I knew there was a family in trouble. I wanted to know what would happen to them. I wanted to do something to help them continue on their way and finally escape from slavery.

Most of the people who passed through our station on the Underground Railroad were heading for Philadelphia, Pennsylvania. There are lots of Quakers in Philadelphia, and Quakers are passionately against slavery. There is an organization in Philadelphia that helps escaped slaves find jobs and new identities. Pennsylvania is a free state, so Negroes want to go there. Some slaves are going on to Ohio, and some are hoping to travel as far as Canada.

What I gathered from eavesdropping on the discussion below me on the first floor was that only the father was expected to come to my grandparents' house to be passed along the Underground Railroad escape route. He had arrived a day late, for whatever reason, and now nobody could go into the tunnel because of flooding from the storm. And, the escaping slave had unexpectedly brought his wife and two children, including an infant, along with him. He was not supposed to bring his entire family. My grandparents' route to freedom was not prepared to deal with four people at this time. But here they were, and who could blame the man for not wanting to leave his family behind? I certainly couldn't fault him, but this presented a huge problem for Gram and Grandpa Doc. Going to the basement and into the tunnel was not an option for the family, or for even one person tonight. It had rained too hard, and the tunnel was too wet. Something else would have to happen.

I also learned from listening through the bannister that one of the slaves thought a gang of plantation owners from Virginia had assembled and was following the family. The slave owners were on their way north to try to capture him and take him back to the plantation. This often happened when someone tried to leave their slavery bonds behind. The plantation owners considered the escaped slaves their own personal property, and slave owners were willing to go to great lengths to get their property back. If there was a party of slave catchers on the way to try to find and recapture this family, that could mean a lot of trouble.

The four escaping slaves couldn't hide in the tunnel because it was flooded, but where could they go? Where would they stay until the water in the tunnel had disappeared or they could otherwise move forward along their route to freedom? Grandpa Doc was telling Gram he didn't want to involve my brother and me in this problem. Gram was saying they had no choice.

"They are too young, and I don't want them put at risk. They will become a part of this soon enough, but tonight is too soon." Grandpa Doc was adamant.

"We don't have a choice. We are going to have to hide these people here, inside our home for tonight and perhaps for several nights. There may be slave catchers searching for them. I'm not willing to give them up without at least trying to hide them, especially with a small child and a baby. I think Joseph and Louisa are old enough to understand what is happening and what they have to do."

"I'm against it, but I don't see that we have another choice." Grandpa Doc was resigned. He knew he'd lost this one to my grandmother.

Gram began to climb the stairs. The family of four followed her up to the second floor. I ran back to my bedroom and pretended to be asleep when Gram pushed open the door to my bedroom.

There was a closet in my bedroom that contained a narrow stairway hidden behind a neatly constructed partition. The partition was so cleverly fitted into the wall and the woodwork that it was impossible to see it. You would never know the panel could be moved if you didn't know where to look. You could find it only by feeling around the edges. The hidden staircase behind the panel led to an attic. It was almost too narrow for a grownup to walk on, and it was steep. My Gram was quiet as she led the family to the closet and whispered to them about climbing up the narrow stairs into the attic. Just as they began to climb to the attic space, the baby began to cry. It was loud in the bedroom, and no one could sleep through the noise. I sat up in bed and looked at my Gram. She rushed the four Negroes up into the third floor attic and closed the panel and the closet door. In addition to the parents and the baby, I had also seen a small boy who looked as if he might be two or three years old.

"Louisa, I have to talk to you about something. It is very important. I've not wanted to bring you into this grownup situation before. I didn't want to involve you in it tonight either, but something has happened. I'm going to have to tell you some things that you're going to have to learn about right now."

"It's okay Gram, I know more about what is going around here than you think I do. I know you're moving slaves to freedom. I know this house is a stop on the Underground Railroad. I think it's wonderful, and I want to help slaves escape, too, to help with the good work you are doing."

My Gram sighed with relief, and I could see the wrinkles on her forehead disappear when I'd told her I already knew their secret and that I wanted to be a part of it. Gram hugged me and told me to go back to sleep. She said she would explain it all in the morning. I told her I knew there was family with a baby in the attic over my bedroom. She hugged me again and said we would talk later.

But I would have to participate in the plot before morning came. I never expected that slave catchers would really come to my grandparents' house and force their way inside, but that's what happened later that night.

Four men on horseback arrived at the house about three o'clock in the morning. They had ridden hard and fast to get to the doctor's house in Burley, and they were loud. I woke up and looked out the window of my bedroom. I could see them standing on the walk in front of the house. They were shouting for my grandparents. One of the men carried a lighted torch, and I thought one of them was holding a long gun. They were angry and looked mean and rough. Two of them climbed the steps onto the porch and pounded on the front door. Grandpa Doc and Gram had apparently been expecting them. The men kept banging on the door. I crept out onto the second floor landing again and listened through the railings of the staircase to the threatening conversation that was taking place below me on the first floor.

"We know they were heading here. We know what your sympathies are. We know you help slaves escape their masters. You know it is against the law for you to do that. We know you can tell us where to find them. They are our property. You have no right to hide them from us. We are here to take them back where they belong."

"I have no idea what you're talking about. There are no slaves here. Leave my house at once. I will call the sheriff and have you thrown out." My Gram was pretty good at lying about the slaves being in the house, and she was brave to stand up to this group of aggressive men.

One of the men took a revolver from the pocket of his coat and waved it in my grandmother's face. I didn't think he would shoot her, but it was scary to see someone put a gun to her head. I was frightened for her, but my grandmother acted as if she wasn't frightened at all. She stood her ground and tried to force the men backwards and out of the house. One of them pushed her aside, and she fell to the floor. Not one of the men stepped forward to try to help her up. She was strong and tough, but she was an old women. A fall could be a bad thing for an older person. I hoped my Gram hadn't broken any bones. Where was Grandpa Doc? All four men trooped inside and began to look in every possible corner on the first floor of the house. I was afraid for my Gram and for the rest of us. I was especially afraid for the family hiding in the attic.

It wouldn't be long before the men came upstairs to the second floor and were in my bedroom. I wished I could think of something to do. My room was the last one they searched, and I pretended I was asleep when they got to me. I stayed under the blanket with my eyes tightly closed, and they searched and searched my room. They looked in the closet, but they didn't notice the perfectly fitted panel in the wall that hid the attic staircase. Maybe they would leave, and everything would be all right.

Just as I thought they were going to give up and leave us alone, the baby in the attic began to cry. It was difficult to tell exactly from what direction the sound was coming, so I sat up in bed and began to cry. I tried to make my cries sound like those of the baby, and I tried to make my own cries loud enough to be louder than the baby's cries. The group of rough men stared at me and looked around the room. I don't know if I really fooled them with my pretend crying, and they stayed right by my bed and watched me. When the baby finally stopped crying, I stopped crying, too. I hoped I had fooled these mean plantation owners who had pushed my Gram to the floor.

"Where are they hiding? We know they are here some place. You can't fool us. We will keep searching the house until we find them. Come on, little girl, we can get tough with you if you don't tell us what we want to know." The man who seemed to be in charge of the search party approached my bed. I was afraid he was going to grab me and kidnap me. I dived under the quilt and the blankets and tried to disappear. Just as he was about to get to me, there was a loud noise at my bedroom door. I peeked out from underneath my blanket, and there was Grandpa Doc standing at the door with a shotgun in his hands.

"Get out of my house. I don't want to hurt anybody. I'm a doctor, and I am in the business of saving lives, not shooting people. But, if you touch my granddaughter, I will have to shoot you. If you don't get out of my house right now, don't doubt for a minute that I will blast you to Kingdom Come. We don't know anything about your slaves. You will have to look for them in somebody else's house. Maybe they are in the woods. Maybe they died on the journey from your plantation. Who knows? It isn't my problem. Now get out of here, before I lose my patience. I have never shot a man in my life, but maybe tonight will be the first time."

I was terrified. I'd never before heard my grandfather speak like this to anyone. I think the men in the search party were scared, too. They looked at Grandpa Doc with wide eyes, and they looked at each other. Then they turned around and tramped loudly back through the upstairs hall toward the stairs.

The leader of the group of men spoke up as they began to go down the steps. "We will get you one of these days, Doc Taylor. You think you have outwitted us, and maybe you have for now. But we will get you in the end. Those people are our property. We paid good money for them, and they belong to us. You are breaking the law by not returning our slaves to us. You are stealing our assets from us by not giving them up. Mind you! We will be back! We get what is ours, and you will suffer! The law is on our side. Slavery is legal in this country and in the states of Maryland and Virginia. We know our rights. You are the ones who will go to prison. Mark my words! We know your wife is an abolitionist. She is very outspoken, and the whole world knows she is a crusader against slavery. She makes no secret of her views. She'd better watch out. There are lots of people who would like to silence her."

I heard all of this, and I was frightened for both of my grandparents. I thought the men were leaving … at least for now. We had won this time, but I had a feeling there were many more times to come. I thought Gram and Grandpa Doc were extraordinarily brave to stand up for what was right. Until tonight, I'd not fully understood how dangerous the work they were doing really was. My respect for them increased, but my fears for their well-being also increased. They were courageous. I loved them both so much and didn't want anything to happen to them. I lay awake in my bed until dawn, unable to go back to sleep.

CHAPTER THREE

My First Mission

13-25   6-9-18-19-20   13-9-19-19-9-15-14

I slept later than usual the next morning. The delicious smell of pancakes and sausage finally woke me. I dressed quickly and ran downstairs to eat my breakfast. Blueberries were just coming into season, and Celia had made blueberry pancakes. I love blueberry pancakes. We eat them with our own churned butter and syrup from Vermont. The syrup costs a lot of money, but Grandpa Doc loves the taste of real maple syrup and has it sent specially from New England.

Both Gram and Doc looked tired this morning. It was no wonder they were exhausted after all that had happened the night before. My brother had already eaten breakfast and gone out to play. My grandparents had serious expressions on their faces, and I knew they intended to have an important discussion with me.

"Louisa, we need to talk to you about some things that are controversial. You told your Gram last night that you know our family works to move slaves to freedom along the Underground Railroad. We figured it would be almost impossible to hide what we do from you for much longer. You are a smart and observant child, and we have always been proud of the person you are. We're going to share more of our secret lives with you. Your Gram believes you are old enough to help us. I am not in favor of bringing you into this dangerous project we have undertaken. You are only twelve years old, and you should still be able to be carefree and live without adult worries to burden you. But last night, you were rudely thrust into our dangerous world by circumstances. I have to tell you, when I saw those men point their guns at you, I felt sick to my stomach. You are still an innocent, but Gram says you have known about our activities for quite a while. You have kept important confidences better than many adults might have been able to do. I have reluctantly agreed that it is time to bring you into our secret undertaking."

"I have known about all of this for a long time, and I want to help. Please tell me what I need to know and what I can do."

Gram and Grandpa Doc spent more than an hour talking to me at the breakfast table. I knew they were not telling me everything they were involved in, but I was glad they trusted me enough to tell me some of it. They really were going to let me help. This would be my summer's work … to be an agent of the Underground Railroad, to help smuggle slaves to freedom. I was excited and a little bit scared at the same time.

Gram already had an assignment for me for the next afternoon. The family that was in the attic had to be moved out of the house as quickly as possible. They could not all be moved together at the same time. It would be taking too much of a risk to move four people at once. The mother and the baby were leaving tonight by another secret route I wasn't told about. The father and the little boy, who was three years old, would leave with me the next day. It was important that the family get to a schooner that was waiting just off the coast in the Atlantic Ocean. This family would travel to Philadelphia by ship. My job would be to deliver two members of the family to a pier on an inlet north of Burley where another boat would transport them out into the Atlantic to board the schooner.

The Eastern Shore of Maryland has many inlets, bays, and coves. There is water everywhere. My brother and I have a small rowing boat, and over the years we have explored most of the waterways near our farm. We are both excellent swimmers, and we are both excellent rowers. Mama trusts us to take our little boat out on the water alone and to be safe using it. The next afternoon I would use my knowledge of the local waters to help two slaves escape their bondage. My Gram went over and over with me what I was to do. I could tell she was worried about asking me to do this, but I was not nearly as worried as she was. The plan was simple, and I thought I could accomplish what was required of me with no trouble at all.

My grandmother explained to me why she could no longer do this work. "Everybody in the area knows I am an ardent abolitionist. I have never made a secret of what my views are. Because I have chosen to be so outspoken, it isn't possible for me to be as covert about my movements as I would like to be. Slave owners and slave hunters are suspicious of me and are always watching me. On the other hand, you, dear Louisa, are above suspicion. No one will suspect, when they see you on the creek in your little rowing boat, that you have two slaves with you who are making an escape."

I could scarcely sleep that night, thinking about what was going to happen the next afternoon. I knew what I had to do, and I could do it. What could go wrong?

The next morning, I checked my little rowing boat to be sure it was shipshape and ready for its task. I oiled the oar brackets so they wouldn't squeak. Clement was the father who would travel with me, and Amen was his little boy. Gram fed them a big lunch in her kitchen, and Clement and Amen went down to the basement to leave the house through the tunnel. Gram and I walked to the tunnel's entrance near the creek where I had already positioned my boat. The creek had risen as a result of the storm, which was an advantage for the way we intended to smuggle Clement and Amen to the pier.

My boat was small, built for only two people. Clement would make the trip in the water, hanging on to the side of the boat. In June, the water was not that cold in the creek. Amen would ride in the boat with me. He would have to lie down on the floor, and we would strap him in so he didn't fall out. There was a square of canvas that I could pull over him to hide him if anyone approached us. Clement would duck under the boat to hide himself if we met anybody unexpectedly. He had a metal breathing tube so he could stay submerged for a long time. He could go under the water and swim alongside the boat. He would raise the tube above the surface of the water so his body would be hidden below the water. At the same time, he would have air to breathe. It was clever. My Grandpa Doc had fashioned the breathing tube out of a piece of metal pipe, so it was easy for Clement to use if he had to stay under the water.

Gram made sure everyone was positioned where they were supposed to be. Clement was on the side of the rowing boat that was away from the shore and toward the middle of the creek. There would be less chance that somebody would see him that way. Amen was a well-behaved little boy and did what his father told him to do. It was about four-thirty in the afternoon when we set off on our journey down Crooked Creek. We expected it would take about an hour to get to the pier to meet the larger boat. That bigger boat could not traverse the tricky waters of our creek. My little work boat was perfect for this first part of the journey. The draft of its hull allowed it to navigate the shallow shoals of Crooked Creek. We would meet up with the larger boat, a dinghy, at the pier. That dinghy was sizeable enough to transport my two charges out into the ocean to meet the schooner.

Everybody wanted to wait until dark to make this trip, but the schooner had already been waiting off-shore for too long. It had to move on at dusk or it would arouse suspicion. If the schooner was suspected of doing something other than transporting what was listed on its manifest, it could be boarded and searched. If they were found aboard the ship, the slave family would end up in terrible trouble. The captain of the schooner could also be arrested and put in jail. We could not wait for darkness. The ship had to sail before the sun went down. If I couldn't get Clement and Amen to the pier in time for the larger dinghy to take them out to sea, the schooner would sail for Philadelphia without them. Timing was critical.

I rowed and rowed. I did this all the time, so it wasn't hard for me. Amen was lying quietly in the bottom of the boat, and Clement was hanging onto the side. We were fifteen minutes from our rendezvous at the pier when the unexpected happened. Clement saw the flatboat in the distance before I saw it. I knew most of the people who owned boats in the area, and I didn't know who owned this large flatboat. I worried that it might be slave hunters.

Clement was going to have to go under the water and use his breathing tube to avoid being seen by whoever

was on the flatboat. Amen was going to have to be perfectly still and stay underneath the canvas cover so he
couldn't be seen. He was going to have to be absolutely
silent until the danger passed. His father would not be
able to reassure the little boy as he lay covered up in the
bottom of the boat, hiding from the world. I felt as if
my heart was rising into my throat. This was my first
assignment, and we were in trouble.

As I approached the flatboat, I waved and shouted
a greeting to whoever was in the boat. Two big men
were pushing the boat along the opposite bank of the
creek with long poles. I didn't recognize the men. They
weren't from this area, or from any of the towns around
Burley. One of them shouted at me, "We're looking for
two runaway slaves. Have you seen a Negro man and a
little boy anywhere along the bank of the creek?"

I gulped and wondered how in the world the men in
the flatboat could possibly know who I had as passengers,
inside and alongside my rowboat. They had said they
were looking for a man and a little boy. Who could have
given them that very specific information? I shouted
back, "I haven't seen anybody at all since I left home."

"There is a big reward, cash, for anyone who tells us
where these two are hiding."

"I don't know anything about that."

"Where are you going at this time of day, little girl?"

My Gram had prepared me for this moment. "I'm
going to the pier to pick up fresh fish for my family to
have for dinner tonight. The sea bass are running, and

we are going to fry it up." I smiled a big innocent smile and tried to look hungry.

"Keep your eyes out for darkies who might be trying to escape. If they won't give themselves up so we can take them back to their owners, we intend to shoot them on sight."

I wondered if they really meant they would shoot them. It seemed as if the whole point of hunting down the runaways was so they could be returned to work on plantations for the people who thought they owned them. What good would it do to shoot them? Slaves were no good to anybody if they were dead.

I wondered if Clement could hear the men. I pulled the canvas that covered Amen more tightly around his little body. I whispered for him to stay quiet. I was scared.

We finally made it to the pier, but there was no boat waiting there for my two passengers. I had made good time getting to the meeting place, and the larger dinghy should have already been at the pier. Had it left early? What was I going to do? Clement continued to hide under the water, and Amen was being very still under his canvas cover.

I asked myself if I should get out of my boat and look for someone, but I decided to stay in the rowboat with Amen. He might be frightened if I wasn't there. I didn't even know if he knew how to swim. I leaned over the side of my boat and hoped Clement could hear me. "The dinghy isn't here. We're here in plenty of time, so they can't have left yet. I think we should wait a little bit and see if the dinghy shows up." I was beginning to panic. I knew plans hardly ever went exactly as they were expected to go, but this was my first mission. More than anything, I wanted to do everything right, and now I had no idea what I was supposed to do.

I waited for a while, although I knew there was a deadline for my passengers to make it out to the schooner that sat offshore. It wasn't long until my friend Ollie came running down the pier and called out my name. Ollie is my brother's friend, and he's also a friend of mine. His parents are good friends with my mother, and they have a farm near ours. They don't have any slaves working on their farm, just like we don't. I knew I could trust Ollie.

"There's been a change in the plans, Louisa. Move to the bow and let me have the oars. I have to take your boat to a new meeting place, and we have to hurry." I climbed across Amen, who was staying still in the bottom of my little boat. I sat in the bow, and Ollie climbed in and took the oars. My boat was small, and I was worried that three passengers would be too much for it. Fortunately, one of the passengers was only three years old.

Ollie was a strong oarsman, and he knew where he was going. He pulled away from the pier and doubled back down the creek, the way we'd come. He took another inlet off of Crooked Creek, one of the many small channels that made their way out into the Atlantic Ocean from this coastal plain. Ollie put his finger over his mouth, a signal for me not to talk.

A few minutes later, we rounded the bend and found ourselves in a small cove. Ollie rowed my boat directly into a thick grove of vegetation and tree branches that hung out over the water. There, well-hidden in the swamp, was the larger boat that would carry my two passengers to the schooner waiting at sea. Clement, soaking wet from having been swimming in the water alongside my rowboat, scooped up Amen, and quickly climbed aboard the dinghy. Someone was on board to cover them up so he and Amen would not be seen. Black faces out in the open on the deck of any boat could cause serious trouble for everybody.

Ollie immediately began to move my rowboat away from the swamp trees and vegetation. I hadn't had a chance to say goodbye, but the most important thing was that, if nothing else went wrong, it looked as if Clement and Amen would make it to the schooner and would soon be on their way to Philadelphia and freedom as planned.

"Why wasn't the boat at the pier like it was supposed to be?" I hoped Ollie could give me an explanation.

"It was the two slave hunters in the flatboat. They were up here from Virginia and were on the creek looking for the man and the little boy. We couldn't have you transfer them at the pier. We needed a more secret place. I was sent to intercept you, and I almost didn't get there in time. Luckily, you waited a little bit. The men in the flatboat were determined to get hold of your passengers. They knew they were out on the creek someplace. I guess we were lucky this time and outsmarted them."

"How did they know about Clement and Amen? My grandmother was quite secretive about telling me the plans. I didn't think many people knew what was going to happen. The slave hunters knew there was a man and a little boy who were being moved. How could they have known that?"

"Unfortunately, there is always somebody who can be bribed to tell things they are not supposed to talk about. There are spies who are watching those of us they believe are moving slaves to freedom. We have suspected for some time that there is someone who is watching everything we do very closely. It's someone we would never guess who is spying on us. I don't know exactly what happened this time, but I do know those men in the flatboat really wanted to find Clement. He must be a valuable slave. He must have skills. Once he gets to Philadelphia, he should be all right. He will have a new name and a whole new life with his family. The slave hunters will never find him. If he were going on to Canada, nobody would be able to take him back, but there is a group in Philadelphia that does a remarkable job of helping former slaves make new lives for themselves. They will be fine. Don't worry. You look so pale and frightened."

"This is my first assignment. I'd wanted everything to go smoothly. Of course, it never does, but I had hoped. After today, I guess I'm ready for anything to happen, and I've learned I have to be prepared for the unforeseen. I can relax now. Things did not go exactly as we'd hoped, but the family is safe. That's the important thing." When we looked down the creek, we could see the schooner as it hauled anchor and began to move north. Ollie and I smiled at each other. We had accomplished our mission.

CHAPTER FOUR

My Friend
the King of Israel

13-25   6-18-9-5-14-4   20-8-5   11-9-14-7   15-6   9-19-18-1-5-12

My brother was angry that he was missing all the fun and excitement this summer. He was being tutored every day by a special tutor who had been hired by our grandparents to improve his academic skills. Joseph needed extra help to be sure he would be able to keep up with the other students in the class when he entered his new school in the fall. Gram and Grandpa Doc were paying for the tutor and for the school in Washington, D.C. They wanted Joseph to have every opportunity to succeed.

Joseph was jealous that I was being allowed to help smuggle slaves out of Maryland. He didn't like to have to stay inside, reading and studying. He would rather be outside with me, rowing our boat, and doing the exciting things I was doing.

I was exhausted after I stowed my rowboat in the boathouse at the edge of the creek and walked to my grandparents' house in Burley. I was eager to tell them what had happened and that Ollie had helped me. I wanted them to know that the Negroes they had hidden in their attic were now safely on their way north aboard the schooner.

My dress was dirty from dragging in the water. My hair had come loose from my pigtails, and I had lost one of my hair ribbons. But none of that mattered, and I was thrilled that Clement and Amen were going to be free. My mother came to town to have dinner with Joseph and me and Gram and Grandpa Doc. They all wanted to hear my story. I was hungry after all of the excitement, and Celia had made my favorite country fried steak with mashed potatoes and gravy. She'd also fixed green beans the way I love them, with ham and onions and cooked a long time. There was rhubarb pie for dessert. I ate until I couldn't eat any more. I talked until I couldn't talk any more. I told every detail of what had happened that day.

I told my grandparents and my mother everything the slave hunters had said to me. I told them they'd specifically said that they were looking for a man and a small boy. "How could they know that?" I asked my family members who were sitting at the table. They frowned and looked at each other. They didn't say anything, but I knew they were worried. There had been a betrayal somewhere. Someone was spying on our activities. I thought long and hard about this, wondering who in the world it could possibly be. Joseph was jealous that I'd had an adventure. He glared at me.

Usually, we only bathe in the big tub on Saturday nights, and we take sponge baths the rest of the time. But Gram had a special surprise for me that night. She had hot water ready in the tub at her house, just for me. She knew I would want to scrub myself clean after my mission. She washed my hair with her special soap that smelled like flowers. The water I was sitting in felt so warm and good, I almost fell asleep in the big tin bathtub. I did go to sleep in one of the rocking chairs on Gram and Grandpa Doc's front porch. Somebody carried me to an upstairs bedroom. It had been a very eventful day.

When I woke up the next morning, my Gram gave me the news that Clement and his wife and two children had successfully arrived in Philadelphia. I always wondered how she found out these things so quickly, but I was relieved to hear the family was safe at last. I was proud of the part I had played in helping them to become free human beings. I was eager for another assignment, but I hoped it would be a few days before I was called on to help out again. I needed to rest before undertaking my next mission.

I rode my pony home and worked the rest of the day in my mother's kitchen garden. We were harvesting lettuce and peas, and the green beans were beginning to come on the vines. I begged off in the afternoon, and

Cranky and I fell asleep under the trees as I read my book. This Underground Railroad work was exhausting, but I had loved every minute of it.

Somebody shook me. My book was on the ground. I hadn't meant to fall asleep and was startled when someone woke me up. It was Solomon, who had been my friend and playmate ever since I was born. He and my brother Joseph and I had spent many hours of our lives exploring, fishing, boating, and playing together. Solomon was the son of a slave who lived on the plantation next to our farm. Because his father was a slave, this meant that Solomon was also a slave.

My mother didn't have much to do with her neighbors because they owned slaves. Their cotton plantation was large, hundreds of acres, and they had many Negro slaves. They had a big mansion with lots of outbuildings, and many of their slaves worked in the house. Our neighbors had different views from ours about slavery, and they did not like my mother. They didn't like it that Solomon wanted to come over to our farm and play with Joseph and me, but he did it anyway. My mother was always glad to have him play with us.

The slave owners who live on the big plantation have children, and one of them is a girl named Ava who is about my age. She wears long white dresses with lots of petticoats, and her hair is always perfect. She doesn't like to play outside. I like to climb trees and go fishing and row my little boat. My brother, Solomon, and I love to swim in Crooked Creek. Ava doesn't like to do any of the things we like to do. She wants to stay in the house all the time and play with her dolls and other fancy toys. I like to play with my dolls, too, but I also like to spend time outdoors. Ava only comes outside to sit on the porch of her gigantic plantation house and drink lemonade. She's not a tomboy like I am, so we are not really friends. Also, I think she's kind of mean and uppity. She's not much fun at all. I prefer to spend my time with my brother and with Solomon. We have exciting adventures.

Slaves are not allowed to learn to read and write. It is strictly forbidden. My mother had tutored me at home before I started attending the school in Burley. She still teaches the children of the Negroes who work on our farm. For three hours every morning, she teaches them reading, writing, and arithmetic. She also teaches geography and history. They learn about the American Revolutionary War and look at maps. All the Negroes who live at Elderberry Farm know how to read and write … at least a little bit. My mother was sorry she couldn't also teach Solomon, but he belonged to our neighbors who would never have allowed that.

Solomon has always been remarkably smart and wants so much to learn everything. When we were very young, I secretly began to teach him to read and write. He would meet me in my special reading spot in the woods, and I would teach him something new every day. Even if we just had fifteen or twenty minutes to spend, he always learned something. He was so quick to pick up everything I taught him. I never had to tell him anything twice. He always learned it the first time, and he didn't mind being taught by a girl who was two years younger than he was. He was an eager student. I shared my books with him, and he hid them under his straw mattress in the slave quarters at the plantation where he lived. Even after I started attending school in town, I made time every afternoon to spend with Solomon, to share with him what I was learning at my school. His education was our secret. Solomon and I have been best friends all of our lives.

Solomon turned fourteen at his last birthday, and his master is making him work more and more hours. Solomon is now considered to be an adult, and he is required to do as much backbreaking work in the fields as his father does. Consequently, Solomon doesn't have as much time for learning as he used to have. It's a shame, because he loves his studies so much.

Solomon had been sickly as a child, and he isn't a strong and healthy young man. He is often ill with one thing or another. He has difficulty breathing, especially when the air is hot and humid. He's not a good candidate for working in the cotton fields from dawn until dusk. I know he would rather be reading than plowing. He seems to be tired all the time these days and isn't his usual cheerful self. I can see him growing thinner and thinner, as his work hours have increased. I am worried about him.

My mother is also worried about Solomon, and I suspect she has a plan in mind. My Gram tried to buy

Solomon from his owners, but they turned her down. They knew she would give Solomon his freedom if they sold him to her. Her offer just made them even angrier at my family. I asked my mother one night what we were going to do about Solomon. I told her I was afraid the work in the fields was going to kill him. She hugged me and told me not to worry. She said she was going to take care of it. I trusted that she would, but I hoped Solomon would live long enough for her plan to become a reality.

Meanwhile, my mother told me about the all-important quilts that she and other women in and around Burley were always in the process of making. Quilting is a significant part of the lives of all women, whether they live in town, on a farm, or on a plantation.

We have a big barn for our animals and for the hay, but we also have a smaller quilting barn. This barn is where my mother and her friends have their quilting frame set up and where they work on their quilts, protected from the sun and from the rain. There is even a fireplace in the barn, so the quilters can continue to work, even when the weather is cold. Quilting frames are large and require a lot of space, and some quilts can take years to complete. My mother always has a quilt underway. I can't remember a time when she wasn't working on at least one.

Mama lets me help her cut out the pieces for the quilts. We use scraps of fabric and draw around paper templates to form the shapes that will be sewn together to make the beautiful and colorful quilt patterns. I'm good at tracing around the templates, and I am careful when I use my mother's sharp scissors to cut out the pieces that the women will sew together. Sometimes the pieces are quite small.

This summer my mother is going to teach me how to put the pieces together to make the quilt tops. She will tell me how she decides to put certain colors together to create pleasing designs, and I will learn how to sew the tiny stitches that keep the pieces together. My mother has an artistic eye, and her quilts are the most beautiful in town. My grandmother used to be a gifted quilt maker, but now that she's older, the rheumatism in her fingers keeps her from being able to do the meticulous tracing, cutting, and sewing that is required to make a quilt top.

My grandmother still has a great interest in quilts, and she orders fabric from New York and Boston to be sent to her in Burley. Gram orders cotton prints and beautiful pieces of silk. She buys both sturdy wool tweeds and light-weight soft wools that come from England and Scotland. A seamstress makes some of these bolts of fabric into our clothes. We use the scraps and bolts of cotton cloth for our quilts. The colorful and carefully chosen fabrics are one reason our quilts are so wonderful. I love to be at my Gram's house when she opens a package of dry goods that she's ordered from the city. She is always thrilled with whatever arrives. She exclaims with joy and is so excited about each new pattern and texture. She touches the cloth and rubs it between her fingers. I'm sad she can't make quilts any more.

After the pieces for the quilt tops have been sewn together, the three parts of the quilt are assembled. The top is layered with the soft cotton inside of the quilt and the back of the quilt, which is usually a large piece of cotton in one solid color. This bottom layer, the reverse or back side of the quilt, is often white, but it can be any color. My mother puts all kinds of bright solid colors on the backs of her "special" quilts. Then the actual quilting begins. The women stretch the three layers of the quilt out and secure them inside the wooden quilt frame with small screws that are all around the edges of the frame. These quilt layers have to be pulled tight enough so that the women can sew through all three layers of fabric at once. They take many, many tiny stitches and "quilt" the layers of fabric together … the patterned top, the soft lining, and the back of the quilt. The result is a magnificent work of art, a picture full of color and energy that also can be used on our beds at night. It's a wonderfully creative process, and I can't wait to be more a part of it.

In addition to keeping us warm during the winter months, there has always been something special about some of our quilts. My mother keeps most of our quilts in the bedrooms where we use them when it's cold. But she keeps others, the ones we hardly ever use, in a closet near the back door. Our back door opens onto a wide yard that slopes down toward the water. Our household helpers hang the washing on clotheslines that we've put up in the yard. I've also noticed that sometimes my mother will hang one or more of her special quilts on the clotheslines. The quilts are not wet and don't need to be put out in the sun to dry. When I've asked my mother about this, she's told me she puts the quilts on the line to "air out." Since we don't ever use them, I've wondered why they need to smell like fresh air.

When I got a little older I realized that hanging the quilts on the line was of much more importance than just to air them out. The quilts my mother chose to hang on the line were purposely placed there to send critical messages to some of our neighbors. Our back yard, because it is large and on the creek, can be seen by many neighboring farms and homes. Neighbors from fairly far away can see the quilts hanging on our clothes lines. Boats that row up and down the creek can see what is hanging outside behind our house. This summer my mother is going to tell me everything that is going on with the quilts. She's going to teach me about the quilt code.

CHAPTER FIVE

Learning the Code

12-5-1-18-14-9-14-7   20-8-5   3-15-4-5

My mother has told me that hanging quilts on a clothes line has long been a way, for those who help move slaves to freedom through the Underground Railroad, to communicate with each other. Because slave holders and slave hunters quickly catch on to the fact that quilts are being used as signals, the code, by necessity, has to be complex and always changing. The code has to be transformed continuously over time, and nothing can be written down. It all has to be kept in our heads.

My mother knows I have a good mind and a good memory. I learn everything quickly, and once I've learned something, I don't forget it. She told me she was preparing me to take over her job as a worker for the Underground Railroad. My Gram had been an organizer, but she is getting older. Her rheumatism keeps her from moving around as quickly as she used to. More importantly, everyone in town knows of her strong anti-slavery views. She was born and raised as a Quaker in Boston where she lived before she married Grandpa Doc. There aren't any Quaker Meetings in Burley, so now she attends the Episcopal Church with my grandfather. Gram has continued to speak out against slavery, and people who disagree with her have said that, because she is a northerner, she doesn't understand the ways of the South. She's married to the only doctor in town, so people have to be polite to her. Slave owners, who want slavery to remain a way of life and the law of the land, dislike my Gram very much.

My mother has taken over from Gram as an organizer on the Underground Railroad. Because of the prime location of our farm, and the fact that our back yard can be seen by so many other farms, the clothesline behind our house has become a communications center. My mother, because she's chosen to teach the Negroes who work for us how to read and write, has also made slave owners in Burley and the surrounding area angry. Neither my mother nor Gram are able to do much of anything anymore that has to be done in secret. Everything they do is carefully scrutinized. They have to be extremely careful and are not happy about this. This notoriety is the price they've had to pay for speaking out about what they think is right.

My mother hated to bring me into the actual work of the Underground Railroad at my young age, even though she knows I am mature and smart. She didn't want to put me in danger, but she really had no choice. There were days when neither she nor Sally could put the quilts on the line. Sally is my mother's housekeeper and good friend. Even though she is a Negro, Sally and my mother are close. Sally does work around our house and helps my mother with everything. I know that Sally also helps with the Underground Railroad.

Because my mother runs our farm alone, without a husband, she relies a great deal on Sally's help. There are times when my mother has to travel by herself to Salisbury, Maryland or even as far away as Princess Anne, Maryland to negotiate for the sale of crops or livestock. Sally always takes care of things at the house when my mother makes long trips. But my mother and Sally can't do it all, and they need my help. I'm eager to learn what my mother has to teach me. I'm not afraid to learn and use the quilt code.

I know my mother and Sally go out at night while I'm asleep, to talk to other friends of freedom who share the secrets of the quilt code. The women have to be discreet as they communicate with others about how the code is going to work and how it is going to change over time. One day I will be included in these secret meetings.

Colors mean different things on different days of the week. And every week, the combination of colors and what they mean changes. The code, our signals, change daily and weekly. The code has to change constantly or the slave owners, slave traders, and slave hunters would be able to figure it out. They all know signals are being sent using quilts, but they don't know how the code changes over time. At least we hope they don't know.

There are a few things about the code that never change. A solid red quilt means there is danger. No slaves are to be moved at all if there is a solid red quilt on the line. Everyone is to remain in place, staying well-hidden until it is safe for a passenger to move on to the next "station" on the Underground Railroad. When the solid blue quilt is put out, that is the all-clear signal. This soft grey-blue is my favorite color, and it is a restful, healing shade. Blue means good news in the quilt code. The all-black quilt means that there had been a death, and help is needed. Fortunately, my mother has never had to use her black quilt. We hope she will never have to.

Ordinary, everyday quilts are put on the clothesline to "air out" for real. These colorful, patterned master-pieces are sometimes hung out just as decoys, as red herrings, to confuse those who are trying to decipher the quilt code. My mother puts out her most colorful quilts several times a week, even if nothing is happening with the Underground Railroad. She always has a smile on her face when she puts out the quilts that have no special meaning and are intended to mislead the slave hunters who are trying to figure out our secrets.

The week my mother began teaching me about the code, we put out a green solid background quilt on the line beside a yellow and white flowered quilt. We hung these on the clothesline on a Wednesday. Our green quilt meant we had one person who needed to be moved along the Underground Railroad route. The flowered yellow and white quilt pattern meant it was a young woman who was able to walk on her own to freedom. This time, we happened to have that much information about our next passenger. Sometimes we didn't know anything at all about who was coming our way and would be needing "a ride." If we'd also had a young child accompanying an adult, and that child was too young to walk very far on his or her own, there would have been a pink and blue flowered quilt hung on the line alongside the yellow and white flowered one. It was complicated. If we'd hung the quilts out on a Thursday, the colors and the patterns would all be different from those used on Wednesday. Next week, the patterns and the colors will rotate and mean something else again. My mother and Sally know it all by heart. My mother has said I will know it all by heart soon, too.

Some of the quilts are heavy, too heavy for me to lift onto the clothesline by myself. My mother sometimes puts quilts on the line by herself, but most of the time Sally helps her. I will not be expected to do anything with the quilts by myself for a while because I am still in training. Only in an emergency would I be expected to participate in sending messages via the quilt code.

I've thought a lot about the way the code works. I know I am not allowed to write anything down, that it all has to stay inside my head. It's too dangerous to put anything down on paper. I've tested myself over and over again with possible combinations on different days of the week and from one week to the next. I have asked my mother a hundred questions. She doesn't get angry or impatient with me. She is thrilled I wanted to learn it all and that I'm an enthusiastic participant in this important work.

We've even invented a game that we play in the evenings after dinner. The game is a way for me to learn the code. My mother will tell me that certain quilts are hanging on the line on a certain day of the week, and I try to guess what message the quilts' colors and combinations are attempting to communicate. I have become an expert at the game, and my mother has told me she thinks I not only understand the code but am almost ready to put the right quilts on the line.

Not all of the neighbors are participants in the Underground Railroad. My mother never mentions anybody by name, but she told me about three helpers who live nearby. All of them can see our backyard and what is hanging on the clothesline.

"One of our helpers is a man who can't see our back yard from the house where he lives. But he walks with his dog by the creek almost every day, and he fishes in the creek. If it is too cold or rainy to walk the dog or fish, he might come to the house to buy some of our goat milk soap."

"Oh, I know who that is. That's ...." Before I could say the name of the man with the dog who liked to fish and liked our soap, my mother put her finger to her lips and shook her head. No names were ever to be mentioned out loud. This was for everybody's protection. No names.

"Another friend of freedom lives across the creek and can easily see our back yard. She put quilts on her own clothesline to let me know she has received my messages. She lets me know it is safe to bring an escaping slave through her property or leave that person at her house. Because her farm is on a point of land that sticks out into the water, she also sends signals to boats on the water."

"It sounds as if every time a slave is being smuggled to freedom, there is a different plan. How do you keep it all straight?"

"There has to be a different plan every time. Every passenger list and every trip is different. Sometimes there is a family with small children traveling with us. Sometimes it is just a man alone. We had a group of six children arrive unexpectedly one night. Their parents had died, and they were going to be separated and sold at auction. They were desperate to escape their plantation. We hid some of them for a while. We sent some north on the water. We sent two of them in an ox cart overland to Delaware and points north. It was unusually complicated to move them all. Some of the children were quite young. But in the end, we managed to successfully move them all to freedom, and eventually, they were miraculously reunited. It took several weeks to accomplish all of this, but we managed. We have many friends who secretly and quietly help us move slaves to freedom. Not everyone is as outspoken about their hatred of slavery as your Gram."

"So there are people who help us, even though they don't publicly say they are against slavery?"

"Oh, yes, there are many who want to help in secret. You will get to know these people. Many are your neighbors. We use quilts because everyone has them. All of those who help are not as prosperous as we are. People who are poor, whites and Negroes both, also care about our cause. A quilt represents a large investment of time, but not necessarily a large investment of money. A quilt hung over a fence or on a clothesline is an easy way for us to communicate with each other. A quilt that keeps one warm at night can also save a life."

"I know Ollie's family believes as we do. Ollie helped me with Clement and Amen."

"We don't like to use names. The less we know and say names out loud, the better. If one of us is arrested by the authorities, or worse, picked up and tortured by slave hunters, we don't want to know any names that can be revealed. Many people in the South have invested large portions of their financial assets in the owning of slaves. The total amount of money that's invested in slave ownership in the South is enormous. It is legal to own slaves in Maryland and Virginia. We are working to change that, but until we do, the slave owners have the law on their side. They can rightfully claim their 'property,' their runaway slaves, if they're caught."

"But once they get to freedom, they're all right, aren't they?"

"In most cases they are. But the Fugitive Slave Act of 1850 allows slave owners and slave hunters to go to free states and bring slaves back to the slave states. That is, if they can find them, once they've escaped, slave owners and their agents can legally go to Pennsylvania and bring back their property. Even when slaves have escaped from states where slavery is legal and reached a state where they are free, theoretically, they are still in danger. According to the Fugitive Slave Act, ordinary citizens, just like us, are required to return runaway slaves to their owners or to their owners' representatives. The law demands that everyone assist in the recapture of slaves and return them to their plantations. It is illegal to aid, protect, or hide runaway slaves. We believe it is God's will that people be free, and by participating in the work of the Underground Railroad, we have chosen to join with others in an important act of civil disobedience. The only way for escaping slaves to be completely free and out of danger is to go all the way to Canada. Slavery has been illegal there since 1833. Once a slave has made it to Canada, he or she cannot be brought back to be a slave in the United States."

"But most slaves don't go as far as Canada, do they?"

"Most don't. They stay in Philadelphia or New Jersey or New York. Many go to Ohio and Massachusetts. Part of what we do is to provide escaped slaves with new identities and new names. If they don't want to go as far away as Canada, they know they have to be careful and watch out for slave hunters who are paid to track them down and return them to their masters. We do a good job of helping slaves change their names once they make it to the free states, but our system is not perfect. Sometimes they are caught and taken back to bondage. There is an excellent network that protects escaped slaves in Philadelphia. A man named William Still is important in the Philadelphia Anti-Slavery Society. Quakers and free Negroes who live in Philadelphia assist escaped slaves by providing them with money, clothes, and employment."

"But Mama, it's wrong to return escaped slaves to bondage. Once freedom seekers are in a free state, they deserve to remain free."

"Of course we feel that way, but you know slave owners regard Negroes as their property. They will often go to great lengths and do terrible things to get their property back."

CHAPTER SIX

Freedom for Solomon

6-18-5-5-4-15-13   6-15-18   19-15-12-15-13-15-14

ne day in early July, my mother told me plans were being made to move Solomon along the Underground Railroad to Philadelphia. A family in that city had agreed to take him and keep him safe. He would have a new identity and would attend a school with an excellent reputation. I should have been overjoyed to hear this news, but I began to cry. My mother put her arms around me. She understood that the news about Solomon being able to have his freedom would be both happy and sad for me. I would miss him so much. He had been a part of my life ever since I could remember.

"I understand this is bittersweet for you, to hear that Solomon is leaving. But think about what it will mean for him. He won't have to work in the fields any more. He won't be exhausted all the time. He will have a welcoming family to make sure he has plenty of good food and is treated kindly. He will attend school and have the best medical care available to anybody. The father in his new family is a doctor … like Grandpa Doc. It will be a whole new wonderful life for Solomon."

I tried to look at the bright side, and in my heart, I really was happy for Solomon. But I was sad for me. "Tell me how I can help with his journey." I was trying very hard to be brave.

"He will leave a week from tomorrow. That will be on a Sunday. Everyone will be in church, except for you and Solomon. I will tell anybody who asks that the reason you aren't in church is because you are in bed with a summer cold. This will all be up to you, Louisa. You and Solomon will be on your own for most of the way. You'll drive him in the pony cart. The back of the cart will be loaded with burlap bags full of potatoes and cabbages, and Solomon will be hidden inside one of the burlap bags. It won't be an easy or comfortable trip for him, but you will be able to talk to him and reassure him during the journey." My mother looked at me to see if I was listening and taking in all this information about how difficult the trip would be for me and especially for Solomon.

When I nodded my head to let her know I understood, she continued. "You will have to drive the pony cart a long way, and you and Solomon will be alone. You'll have to take a circuitous route part of the way, and you will deliver him to a farm south of Georgetown, Delaware. After you had driven him to the farm, someone will pick him up there and take him on the next leg of his escape route. It will be a dangerous trip, and it will be exhausting for both of you. Do you think you can do it?"

"I will do anything I can for Solomon." I often drove my pony cart. It required only one horse to pull it. The cart was really a small wagon with four wheels. It had a seat in the front, and space for a limited amount of cargo behind the driver. I usually didn't drive it a long way, but I thought I could drive it as far as Georgetown, Delaware, if that's what I had to do to save Solomon.

"I really don't want to ask you to do this. You are much too young to undertake this kind of mission, but we are all terribly concerned about Solomon's health. If he is forced to work in the fields any longer, we're afraid he will become mortally ill. He has never had strong lungs, and he is failing rapidly. Grandpa Doc is so worried about him. He's the one who has said Solomon must get to freedom immediately. Gram has been working with William Still, that man in Philadelphia I told you about who does important work to help escaped slaves. The two of them have found a family in Pennsylvania that wants Solomon to live with them. Mr. Still and your Gram have arranged everything. We had to have it all worked out before we could tell him ... or tell you. Grandpa Doc is talking to Solomon about the plan today. Solomon will be sad to leave you, too, but he will die if he doesn't escape the plantation life."

"Georgetown, Delaware is far away from Burley. I've never traveled that far from home by myself. I will have to travel more than thirty miles, and it will take a whole day to get there in the pony cart, even if I don't stop. I will have to spend the night in Georgetown and come back the next day."

"Yes, it will take you all day to get to Georgetown, but once you have arrived, there is an excellent network there that will get Solomon the rest of the way to Philadelphia very quickly. It's this part of the journey, between Burley, Maryland and Georgetown, Delaware, that is dangerous and uncertain. You are the only person who can do it. If there were any alternative, I would not even think of allowing you to help. If it were anyone but Solomon, whose life is at risk, I would never consider asking you to do this."

"I can do it. But what will I do when I have delivered Solomon to where he needs to go? Where will I stay in Georgetown? Do we know anybody who lives there?"

"Grandpa Doc can't drive the pony cart with Solomon hidden inside. Everyone would see him and suspect that he was up to something. But your grandfather will ride his horse to Georgetown next Friday. He has a meeting there with some other doctors, so he will be in Delaware ahead of you. As soon as you have safely delivered Solomon to the next station on his route to freedom, Grandpa Doc will meet you. He will take care of everything from then on. But first you have to get Solomon to the farm outside of Georgetown."

"You'll have to draw me a map. I've never been to Georgetown by myself before, but I'll do my best."

"We will study the map beforehand so you know it by heart. You are my brave girl, and I love you so much. We think it's best if Solomon stays close to the plantation until it's time for him to leave. We don't want anything to go wrong. There's someone spying on us, and we think that person is connected in some way with the plantation where Solomon is a slave. We can't have anybody learn of our plans to save Solomon, so he's not going to leave the plantation at all for the next week. You won't see him or be able to play with him. I know that is a disappointment to you, but I think it is for the best. It's the only way to keep him safe."

I knew my mother was right, but it made Solomon's imminent departure even more poignant. The next time I would talk to him, he would be inside a potato sack in the back of the pony cart. I might never actually see his face during that ride. I started to cry again.

I was always reading a book, and right now, I was reading a book called *Vanity Fair* by William Makepeace Thackeray. My Gram had ordered it sent from Boston, especially for me. She knows how much I love to read, and she frequently orders books for special occasions. I love the story of Becky Sharpe's adventures, and I plan to spend extra time reading this week. If I'm not working in my mother's gardens or sewing quilt pattern pieces, I'll be reading *Vanity Fair*. It will be a good way to escape the real world. I won't allow myself to be afraid because of the mission I am about to undertake, and I will not allow myself to cry too much about saying goodbye to Solomon.

Sunday morning arrived all too soon. My mother woke me at four in the morning. I dressed quickly and grabbed the small carpet bag I'd packed the night before. It held two changes of clothes. I planned to be away from home for only one night, but just in case, I'd included some extra things. I packed my book, my hair brush, and my nightgown. My mother was organized and helped me decide what I needed for my overnight trip. I'd traveled with my mother and Gram to visit my cousins who lived in the District of Columbia, but I'd never been away from home overnight by myself. Grandpa Doc would arrange a place for me to sleep in Georgetown, so I wasn't really going to be all alone in a strange place. I was excited and more than a little bit scared.

My mother prepared a big breakfast for me. I love fried potatoes and bacon, and she made me a plate full. I also had fresh peaches, biscuits with butter and blueberry preserves, and a cup of coffee that was half milk. Mama had also packed a lunch basket with ham sandwiches and a roasted chicken. Solomon loves ham sandwiches, so my mother had made plenty of them for our picnic. There were tomatoes and pickles and cucumbers in vinegar, and she'd put in two kinds of cookies. Along with the basket of food, there was a jug of water that Solomon and I would share.

Sally brought the pony cart from the barn. Our work horse, Ithaca, was harnessed to the cart. I knew this mission was important if my mother was going to allow her best work horse to pull the pony cart today. Ithaca was strong and fast, as work horses go, and she always obeyed commands. I felt more than a little bit of relief that I had such a good horse to help me take Solomon part of the way to his new home.

I knew Solomon was already somewhere in the cart. My mother and Gram had told me I could talk to him when no one else could hear me. They had carefully chosen places for us to take breaks on our journey, and they'd also found a place where we could stop to eat our lunch undisturbed. They knew the route well, and they knew the locations that were uninhabited, places that were safe to stop along the road where we could hide the cart and no one would see us.

Sally hugged me, and my mother held on to me for a long time. "I'll be fine." I knew she was worried about me, and I wanted to reassure her. "I will be in Georgetown before you know it. This is important to me, and I am thrilled to be able to help." I smiled at Mama and at Sally. I was still scared, but I didn't want them to suspect how uncertain I really felt.

Whenever I drove the pony cart, my dog Cranky always rode beside me on the driver's seat. Today, I didn't pick her up and put her in the cart with me as I usually do. She didn't understand why she couldn't go along on this trip and started to bark at me. I tried to talk to her and tell her why she couldn't go with me today. She tilted her head to one side, and I could swear she was listening to what I said. Finally she sat down beside my mother. Her ears were down, and she stared at me with a disappointed face.

I gave Ithaca the signal to start and waved to Sally and my mother who were standing in the lane with Cranky. Solomon, Ithaca, and I were off on our adventure into the unknown. It was about five in the morning when we left. We were leaving early so we would be well away from Burley before anybody woke up on this summer Sunday morning. We didn't want anyone to see us ride away.

CHAPTER SEVEN

On the Way to the Promised Land

15-14   20-8-5   23-1-25   20-15   20-8-5   16-18-15-13-9-19-5-4   12-1-14-4

"Solomon, are you back there someplace?"* We were barely out of sight of Elderberry Farm when I spoke to Solomon.

"I'm here and tryin' not to move much. It's real hot and scratchy in this burlap bag, and I can only dread how bad it will be by noon. I'm not complainin', though. I know everybody is takin' a lot of chances to get me away from the plantation. I'm ever so grateful."

"Let me know if you want to stop or want some water. I have a big jug full of water and two tin cups. These dirt roads will be bumpy until we get to the main road, the Dover Road. Then we'll be on a good road for a long way. Once we are on the Dover Road, you won't get bounced around so much. Gram said sometimes it's washed out in places, but for the most part it is made of well-packed dirt and stones. She and Grandpa Doc travel on the road to Dover several times a year. I'll try to make the trip as comfortable for you as possible. My mother has given us her best work horse to pull the cart. That will make the trip much easier. She doesn't let Ithaca pull the pony cart very often."

We rode in silence for over an hour. Several other carriages and wagons passed us on the road. The air was hot and sticky, and I wanted a drink of water from the jug in the worst way. I figured Solomon could also use a drink. I pulled over at one of the stopping places my mother had marked on the map. There was a thick stand of trees, and we were able to pull off the road just far enough so that the pony cart could not be seen from the road.

"I'm stopping for a break, and I think we both need a drink of water from the jug. I'm really hot, and I know you must be, too."

Solomon wrestled his way out of the burlap bag and jumped down from the cart as soon as we stopped. He ran into the woods to relieve himself, and then he came back to get some water. After he'd had a big drink, he walked to the edge of the copse where we were resting. He put his finger to his lips, the signal for me not to talk. I heard a heavy wagon go by on the main road. It was loud and traveling very fast. Solomon was watching from behind a tree as the wagon passed us.

"Louisa, I hate to tell you this, but someone has been followin' us. They've just gone by and don't know we've left the road and stopped to rest. I've been worryin' for a long time, but I'd not had proof that someone at my plantation was spyin' on your family and on me. I should've said somethin' to Grandpa Doc before now, but I didn't want to say anything without bein' sure. Because a wagon full of slave catchers has just passed by on the Dover Road, I know for certain that I was bein' closely watched. Somebody knows everything the Underground Railroad is doin'. They knew I was leavin' today, and they were followin' the pony cart. If we hadn't stopped for a break and hidden ourselves, they could have overtaken us and kidnapped us. They'd have taken me back to my plantation or sold me off to another slave owner … probably far, far away from here. I hate to think what they might've done to you. We were real lucky we stopped when we did."

I was shocked to hear what Solomon had to say, but I knew he was right. Solomon was smart, and he never spoke out about anything unless he was quite sure of his facts. I knew we were lucky that the loud wagon which had just passed by had not been able to overtake us on the road. "I believe you, Solomon, but how do you know all of this? And what are we going to do about it?"

"It's Ava. She's the spy, the one who has been followin' me and listenin' outside the doors and windows of your house on the farm and outside your grandparents' house in town. Everyone thinks she's a precious young lady who stays inside all the time and drinks lemonade on the porch. But I know for certain she sneaks out of the house and spies on people she knows are against slavery. She's dangerous. I have been keepin' my eyes on her for months now, and because I don't trust her, I been very careful about where I go and what I say. I been spyin' on her at the same time she been spyin' on me. Last night, I finally told Grandpa Doc about her spyin'. He didn't believe me at first. Ava always is so polite 'n sweet 'n perfect. But Doc also took precautions. We didn't think anyone knew about my escape and the journey to Georgetown, but we were wrong."

"Ava?" I was stunned that the girl who didn't want to play outdoors and wouldn't get her petticoats dirty was a spy. I knew Solomon would not have mentioned anything to me unless he was absolutely convinced that she was the spy. "If you and Grandpa Doc were so careful, how did Ava find out about today?"

"I don't know, but I do know we're in danger. Is there a different route we can take to Georgetown? Once the wagon full of slave catchers sees they haven't been able to overtake us on the road, they'll come back and search for us. We have to go another way." We opened the map and studied it to try to find an alternative route we could take to the farm near Georgetown. "They can't know where our meetin' place is in Georgetown, where you'll turn me over to the next person on the Underground Railroad. That's one good thing. But we can't stay on the Dover Road. We'll have to take a back road."

I looked at the map and realized the back roads were not good, and the trip was going to take much longer if we couldn't travel on the Dover Road. And, we would have to stay on this main road until we reached the next turn-off. We could only hope that we could get off the Dover Road before our enemies found us. We got back into the pony cart, and I cracked the whip for Ithaca to go faster. I didn't ever actually hit Ithaca with the whip, but she knew the sound of the whip slapping against the side of the wooden cart meant she had to hurry up.

We raced down the Dover Road and turned off when we got close to the Village of Sandy Branch. We couldn't go through the center of the village, so we had to take a narrow, rough dirt road that went around the town. It would be a difficult ride, but I knew Ithaca could do it. I hoped the pony cart would be able to withstand the trip.

We traveled as fast as we could on the tiny road that was little more than a footpath. It was slow going, and I wondered if we would ever make it to the Village of Frankford. That was where my family had told us to stop for lunch. There was a place safe inside a grove of trees were we could hide the pony cart and eat our noon meal. Ithaca could take a rest and there was a pond for her to have a long drink of water. We wandered our way along the narrow back roads. I worried the entire time that we had somehow gotten ourselves going in the wrong direction and were irretrievably lost.

Finally, we arrived at the pond. It was two o'clock in the afternoon. If we'd been able to stay on the Dover Road, we would have arrived here by noon as scheduled. We were two hours behind. Solomon and I were starving. I knew Ithaca was also hot and thirsty. Solomon unhitched the horse from the cart and led her to the pond. She drank and drank … thankful to have water and thankful to be able to stop pulling the cart for a while. I unpacked the basket that held our lunch, and we ate all of the cold chicken and most of the sandwiches. It was hot, and I wanted to take a nap. But we had a long way to go before we could begin to think about letting down our guard.

As we were packing up the lunch and getting ready to resume our journey, we heard a loud clap of thunder. It had been that kind of day, too hot and humid to hold the moisture in the air. We'd known a storm was coming, but we didn't know just when it would break. I had hoped we would be closer to Georgetown before the rain began to fall. The back-road pathways we were following would soon become ribbons of mud. Should we push on and try to travel through the storm, or should we take cover and wait out the deluge we knew was coming? Solomon hurried to harness Ithaca back up to the pony cart. I was tired and decided to take cover under the cart, out of the rain. Solomon had been to the Frankford Village area before and thought he knew of an abandoned barn somewhere close by. I warned him to be careful. I was afraid a Negro wandering around the countryside by himself might attract unwanted attention.

The rain came down hard. The thunder and lightning were fierce. I was all by myself under the pony cart. Ithaca didn't like thunder, and she was getting skittish as well as soaked from the rain. I talked to her to calm her. Solomon and I had covered up the burlap bags of cabbage and potatoes with a big oil cloth. I could have climbed under the oil cloth and stayed dry, but it was too close and too dark under there. I suffered from claustrophobia. It wasn't nice under the pony cart either, but at least I could breathe. I was worried that Ithaca would take off, if the storm made her too afraid. If we we'd been back at the farm in Burley, she would have been safe and dry inside our barn, and I would have been safe and dry inside my house.

Solomon finally returned. He was soaked through to the skin, but he'd found the barn he had been looking for. Most of the barn's roof had fallen in, but there was a part of the barn that still had a little bit of cover over it. It was about a half mile away. Solomon said we should try to get the pony cart and Ithaca and ourselves inside the barn. I agreed with him. I climbed into the back of the pony cart and got under the oil cloth.

Solomon was in the driver's seat, but Ithaca refused to move. She usually obeyed commands without hesitation, so I knew something was wrong. I knew she was spooked by the storm since she usually wasn't left out in the rain. Solomon tugged at her bridle and tried to get her to start walking. She wouldn't budge. Finally, he got down from the pony cart and looked at Ithaca's feet … carefully, one at a time. He found she had a sharp stone imbedded in her left front foot, and it was lodged underneath the iron horseshoe. It was going to be difficult to get the stone out from under the horseshoe, and the horse's foot was bleeding. It had to be painful, so it was no wonder she had refused to walk anywhere. Ithaca was a good horse, and Solomon was good with horses. He worked with Ithaca and finally was able to extract the sharp stone from her foot. Her foot continued to bleed, but the offending stone was gone. She pawed the ground and snorted. The rain continued to come down, harder and harder.

Even though we knew the foot had to still be hurting her, Solomon finally got Ithaca to move. He pulled himself up into the pony cart and urged her onward toward the wreck of a barn. The ground was all mud by now, and it was slow going. Solomon jumped down and opened the doors of the barn. I climbed into the driver's seat and drove the cart inside. Solomon closed the doors behind us. We stayed under the part of the barn that still had a piece of a roof over it. Solomon unharnessed Ithaca from the pony cart to let her roam around the inside of the barn. There was some hay in the loft, although it was anyone's guess how long it had been there. Solomon offered the hay to Ithaca who was happy to have it. We decided to wait in the barn until the storm ended. We still had miles to go before we reached Georgetown, but thought it was better not to be traveling outside in a bad storm.

The wind whipped around the sides of the barn, and the rain poured in where the roof was gone. We huddled in the one dry corner and waited for the rain to stop. Thunder crashed much too close to the barn, and we knew the lightning would also strike close by.

CHAPTER EIGHT

Fire and Rain

6-9-18-5   1-14-4   18-1-9-14

t was our bad luck that lightning did strike. The crack of thunder was deafening. We struggled to hang on to Ithaca to keep her from charging the barn doors to break out. The terrifying moments kept on coming, one after the other without remorse. The lightning struck something in the hayloft of the barn. There was no roof over most of the barn, so the lightning was free to hit us at will. We saw it strike the straw but hoped against hope that the straw was too wet to catch fire. But we did not get our wish. The fire started, and then it seemed to go out. But the fire must have found a dry patch of straw and reignited. In a few seconds, there was a full-blown conflagration, and we knew we had to escape. The flames moved so fast. We thought we had time to get the pony cart out of the barn, and we might have. But one of the wheels of the cart was stuck in the ground. If we'd had a chance to harness Ithaca back up to the cart, she might have been able to pull it free. We didn't have time to do any of that, and we had to move immediately ... to save ourselves and our horse.

Solomon threw open the doors of the barn. The fire burned all around us. Solomon grabbed my carpet bag and his own small bundle of belongings from the back of the pony cart, and I grabbed the picnic basket. The water jug would have to stay behind. Solomon picked up the horse's reins and tried to pull Ithaca outside. But she was terrified, mesmerized by the fire. I got beside her and tried to push her, but that did no good. Solomon threw my carpet bag and his bundle of things at me. He pulled some rags from under the seat of the pony cart, climbed up on Ithaca's bare back, and tied the rags around her eyes. If she couldn't see the fire, we might have a chance of getting her out of the barn.

The blindfold seemed as if it was going to work, but the fire was drawing closer and closer to where Ithaca stood. Solomon screamed at me, "Get out of the barn now. I'm goin' to ride her out." I gathered up our things and the picnic basket. I ran outside into the rain. It seemed like I stood there for ages, waiting for Solomon and Ithaca to appear. The barn was fully engulfed in flames by now. I thought I was going to be sick to my stomach. I was afraid I was going to lose my friend and my mother's best horse in the fire, and there was nothing I could do to help them.

At last, Solomon appeared in the doorway of the barn, riding Ithaca bareback and yelling at her to run. She was wild. She couldn't see, and she was panicked. Solomon rode her away from the fire and then around and around in the woods until she began to calm down. Solomon removed the blindfold from Ithaca's eyes. We were all soaked with rain. My carpet bag and Solomon's little bundle were wet. The picnic basket was sodden. The pony cart was burning inside the barn. Our jug of water and the mugs were in the pony cart. But we were alive, and we were safe.

Solomon reminded me that the fire would bring neighboring farmers to the scene. We had to get out of the area as quickly possible. He pulled me up behind him onto the horse. He jumped off and secured our bundles to Ithaca's harness. We left the picnic basket behind. Ithaca didn't like having anything attached to her harness, and she bucked and reared. When Solomon was able to calm her down again, he climbed up behind me. I was the better horsewoman, so he wanted me in front to try to ride Ithaca with both of us on her bareback. We never rode our work horses. They were not bred for it, and they were not used to having people ride on their backs. Thank goodness we had Ithaca. She was a smart horse and a well-behaved horse. When I took hold of the reins, I finally felt as if I had control over her. We urged her to go as quickly as she could down the muddy road, away from the burning barn.

Ithaca was not a very fast horse, and the roads were worse than they'd been before it started to rain. The wind was blowing the rain sideways, and we could scarcely see where we were going. Ithaca protested but eventually seemed resigned to having us astride her back. I had folded the map and put it inside my carpetbag. I hoped it was still dry. It was raining too hard now to get the map out to check our location. The map was made of paper and would have been destroyed if I'd tried to look at it in the rain. I would have to trust my memory and try to visualize where the roads went and which ones we were supposed to take. Thank goodness I had spent so much time looking at the map during the week before this trip. I'd told Mama I thought I knew the map by heart. I could only hope I had been telling her the truth.

It was completely dark by now, and the rain continued to pour down on us. The road was nearly impassible, and I didn't know whether or not we were actually going in the right direction. It was so hard to see anything. Even if we had managed to stay on the road, was it the right road? Were we still headed for Georgetown?

It was a huge relief when Solomon said he thought we were in Dagsbury. It used to be called Blackfoot Town, after the Indian tribe that lived in the area. Solomon had been there before and recognized it when we got to a cluster of farms outside the town. At least we were heading north, in the direction of Georgetown. We were both exhausted and still had miles to go before we reached our destination.

It continued to rain hard, and the road was slippery. I was allowing Ithaca to go at her own pace, as slowly as she wanted to go. But she took a bad step, slipped in the mud, and went down hard. We both fell off the horse and landed on the ground. We were terrified that Ithaca might have broken a leg. A broken leg was a death sentence for any horse. That was the first thing we thought of ... before we even thought about ourselves. Solomon had fallen underneath Ithaca, and his leg was twisted in an unnatural position. When he tried to stand up, he collapsed on the wet ground. He cried out in pain and said he thought he might have broken his leg. When I looked at it, his leg looked all wrong. It was bent at an odd angle. I almost broke down and cried. I wondered what else could possibly go wrong on this terrible night.

I couldn't leave Solomon there. Somehow I had to get Ithaca upright and get Solomon back on the horse. I had to deliver him to the farm south of Georgetown. That was the reason for this journey, and I refused to allow all that we had endured so far to have been in vain. I was determined to save Solomon, no matter what.

I struggled to get Ithaca to stand. Once she was finally back on her feet, she seemed all right. I didn't think she had any injuries. But Solomon was in terrible pain. He tried hard not to cry out, and he did everything he could to help me as I attempted to hoist him up onto Ithaca's back. He fell backwards onto the ground several times before we finally got him on the horse. I climbed up behind him and held the reins. I also had to hold on to

Solomon to keep him from falling off. As we rode on, he was beginning to lose consciousness, probably from the pain of his broken leg. I was afraid if I didn't hang onto him, he would pass out and slip off the horse onto the ground. I couldn't allow that to happen.

Our progress was terribly slow. It seemed as if we had been on the road for days and days, rather than hours. My mother had described in detail the house where I was to go, and I had a picture in my mind of what that farm house must look like. As we rode along the back roads, all of the farms and farm houses began to look the same. I even approached one farm that looked like the right one, but at the last minute I decided it was not the place we were looking for. We rode on.

At last, I saw a barn that had the doors wide open. I thought the house next to it looked like the place where we were supposed to meet Grandpa Doc and where Solomon was to meet up with the people who would take him to the next station on the Underground Railroad. As we approached the barn, I caught a glimpse of what I was sure was Grandpa Doc's horse in the first stall. Her name is Darling, and she is pure white with a black star on her forehead. I had never been as happy to see a horse as I was to see Darling that night.

I led Ithaca into the barn and put her in an empty stall. I gently helped the barely conscious Solomon slide off the horse and down onto the straw. I made sure he was at one side of the stall where Ithaca wouldn't step on him. I gave Ithaca some food and water. I found a jug of water and some tin cups and tried to get Solomon to drink. He swallowed a little bit, but most of the water rolled out the sides of his mouth and down his chin. When I was satisfied that Solomon and Ithaca would be safe, I went in search of Grandpa Doc. I was dead on my feet and had to make myself keep walking as I tried to reach the farm house.

I fell against the door and pounded with both my fists. I waited and waited. The house was white and the door was red. It seemed like it was a long time before anybody came. A man I didn't know finally opened the red door. I stepped over the threshold and collapsed into his arms. That was the last thing I remembered until the next day.

Grandpa Doc told me later that he had been right behind the stranger who had answered the door. The stranger was the owner of the farm and the house where I had collapsed. I was shaking with the wet and cold, and the farmer's wife and Grandpa Doc carried me into the kitchen to get warm. They asked me where Solomon was, and although I don't remember answering them, I guess I was able to communicate in some way that he was in the barn. The farmer and Grandpa Doc went to take care of Solomon, and the farmer's wife took care of me. She took off my wet clothes and wrapped me in a warm blanket. She tried to rinse the mud out of my hair, and she helped me to a small first-floor bedroom at the back of the farmhouse. The farmer's wife gave me a clean nightgown to wear and left a cup of water on the table beside my bed. I don't remember any of this, but they told me all about it the next day.

Meanwhile, the farmer and Grandpa doc had found Solomon and Ithaca. The farmer made sure the horse was all right, and Grandpa Doc looked at Solomon's leg. Both men were very concerned about him. He did have a broken leg, and by this time, he was delirious. Grandpa Doc was afraid he had an infection or pneumonia from being outside in the rain for so long. My grandfather set and splinted Solomon's leg and tried to make him drink some water. The family who owned this farm had a special compound underneath their barn where they hid slaves who were passing through Delaware on their way to Philadelphia. The farmer and Grandpa Doc carried Solomon down a narrow, winding staircase and got him settled on a cot in one of the rooms of the basement compound. Grandpa Doc insisted on staying all night beside his patient, and he lay down on the cot next to Solomon's.

I didn't wake up until almost noon the next day. When I opened my eyes I saw the farmer's wife. I hadn't remembered seeing her the night before, but she smiled a big smile when I opened my eyes. I could tell she was delighted to see me alive and awake. I smiled back at her. She had a soft and gentle voice. "Welcome to Mayfair Farm. I'm Amanda Mayfair. We were terribly concerned about you and Solomon last night. When you didn't show up on time and with the storm, we were afraid you were lost … or worse. Your grandfather was beside himself with worry. You cannot imagine how relieved he was, how relieved we all were, when you finally pounded on our door. I told Doc he should be strung up for asking someone as young as you are to undertake a dangerous journey like the one you made yesterday."

"How is Solomon?" I didn't want to talk about myself or how scared I had been or how the journey really was almost more than I could handle. I wanted to know how my friend was.

"He has a broken leg, but he's going to be fine. Your grandfather set and splinted the broken leg and tended to him all last night. We will take good care of Solomon and be sure he is safe while his leg heals. Then we will help him continue on his way to Philadelphia. When I scolded your grandfather for sending you on this dangerous trip, he told me he trusted you and Solomon to rise to any occasion and to come through under any circumstances. I guess he knows you both pretty well. I know you have a story to tell, and we all look forward to hearing about your adventure. You must go back to sleep now, and when you wake up, I will have a nice meal ready for you. You are a brave young lady, and we are all proud of you for making it here with Solomon and your horse. Drink some water now and go back to sleep."

It was almost dark when I woke up again. More than anything, I wanted to talk to Solomon, to see him with my own eyes to be sure he was all right. Amanda Mayfair told me Solomon was safely hidden and that it wouldn't be a good idea for him to be seen in the house with us. I was so used to having Solomon around, it took me a few minutes to understand what she was telling me.

Miss Amanda brought me dinner on a tray. There was a big bowl of chicken noodle soup. She had made roast beef and mashed potatoes and gravy for me. There were three vegetables on the plate ... all from their farm garden. I was too full to eat the delicious looking piece of cherry pie, but Miss Amanda put it away for me to eat later. I drank two glasses of milk.

There was a tub of hot water ready for me, and I was so happy to see it. Miss Amanda said she knew, after everything I'd been through, that a tub bath would feel good to me ... even if it wasn't Saturday night. We had to wash my hair three times. It took that much washing to get all the mud out. Miss Amanda said she was soaking the mud out of my clothes. She had cleaned up my shoes but said they were not in good shape. I told her I had almost outgrown them anyway and was going to have to have a new pair soon. I began to feel like myself again, but I kept thinking of Solomon. I wished I could see him.

Grandpa Doc came into my bedroom and sat in the chair beside my bed. He wanted to hear every detail about the journey Solomon and I had made from the farm in Burley. My grandfather told me how worried he had been and praised us for our courage and persistence in making it to Georgetown. When I told him about the wagon full of slave catchers that had chased us on the Dover Road, I could see he was upset to hear that news.

"When Solomon told me he thought Ava was spying on him and on us, I didn't want to believe him. She is such a sweet talker and really knows how to pour on the charm with older people. But I trust Solomon's judgment, and now I know he was exactly right. Ava has been the one who's been eavesdropping on our conversations. She's sneaky, and she passes our plans along to the slave hunters. She is a pretty little snitch. Your instincts were right, Louisa. We wanted you to play with her. Your mother thought maybe being around Ava would convince you to be less of a tomboy. But you knew best, and you didn't want anything to do with her. We are going to have to be exceptionally careful around her from now on. She is good at this spying thing. We never suspected her until Solomon found her out."

"We were supposed to go back to Burley today. Will my mother and Gram be worried when we don't come home as planned?"

"I have sent word to them that we have been delayed. We have no pony cart, so I have borrowed a wagon to take us home to Burley. Ithaca has been through a tough time, too, and she has an injury to her foot. We've had to remove the shoe to allow her foot to heal. I'm worried that her foot might be developing an infection. We have to be very careful about that. The blacksmith will make a new shoe for her after her foot is well again. Solomon told me he had to dig a sharp stone out of Ithaca's hoof. She won't be able to pull a wagon or a pony cart or anything for a while, but I think she will make a full recovery. In the meantime, the Mayfairs have agreed to take care of Ithaca for us."

"She will be all right, won't she, and her foot will heal?" I was feeling guilty that we'd hopped on Ithaca's back and pushed her to continue the journey, even though we'd known she had an injured foot.

"Don't worry, I think she will be fine. But, it will be another day or more before we can get the wagon, and I've also had to borrow two horses to pull it. We're going to stay here at Mayfair Farm until then. I know you are anxious to get home to your own bed, but Miss Amanda and Farmer George have extended their hospitality to us for as long as we want to stay."

I was still so tired, even after sleeping all day. I fell asleep as my grandfather was telling me what the plans were going to be. I knew he wasn't ready to leave Solomon just yet. I was glad Grandpa Doc was taking charge now. Everything was going to be all right.

CHAPTER NINE

Parting is Just Plain Sorrow

16-1-18-20-9-14-7   9-19   10-21-19-20   16-12-1-9-14   19-15-18-18-15-23

The next morning, I found my clothes all clean, dry, and neatly folded in the bedroom wardrobe. Amanda Mayfair had made sure everything I'd brought with me in my carpet bag was washed and ready to wear. I woke early and went to the kitchen to have breakfast with the Mayfairs and Grandpa Doc. But my grandfather wasn't at the table. Miss Amanda had a worried look on her face as she served me a plate of buttermilk pancakes and ham. I knew something was wrong. "What's happened? Is it Solomon?"

"Your grandfather had to do a surgical procedure on Solomon's leg late last night. The bones weren't aligned the way they should have been, and Solomon was in too much pain. Doctor Taylor had been afraid from the beginning that he might have to operate, and last night he finally made the decision. It was a difficult time … especially for Solomon. Your grandfather didn't have time to get hold of any anesthesia to ease the pain for Solomon, but blessedly Solomon was not conscious during most of the surgery. Doc's with Solomon now, and he says the operation was a success. He thinks the broken leg will now begin to heal properly."

I wanted so badly to see Solomon and talk to him. I thought Grandpa Doc would take me to see Solomon if Solomon was not in too much pain to have visitors. "When will Grandpa Doc be back at the house? I need to talk to him."

"He said he would come for breakfast, so we are keeping some pancake batter ready for him. He cares very much for Solomon."

"Yes, he does. He cares very much about all of his patients, but he has a special place in his heart for Solomon. We all do. Solomon is so smart, but nobody wants smart slaves. Slave owners want strong slaves, slaves they can make work in the fields all day long ….backbreaking work from dawn until dusk. They want beasts of burden, really. And Solomon is not one of those. He has never been strong. He has problems with his breathing and really should never have been working in the fields. That's all slave owners want from Negro men, for them to be able to work all day in the fields."

"You know we feel as you do about slavery, but you must be careful where you are when you speak about these things. The Underground Railroad is a dangerous operation. It's best to be discreet."

"I know that, and I know I should not be talking so freely right now. But I am so worried about Solomon. He has been my friend and playmate since we were very young. I am going to miss him tremendously when he goes to Philadelphia."

"I know you will miss him, but you know he has to escape being a slave. He would never survive living a life on the plantation."

"I do know that, and that is why slavery is so terribly wrong. That is why I am as committed as any of my elders to fighting against it."

"We respect your involvement, especially for you to be so active at such a young age. And you do come by it honestly. Those of us who live in Georgetown have a great deal of respect for your family and all they do to help slaves gain their freedom. We especially love reading your grandmother's tracts that speak out so eloquently against slavery."

I didn't know what she was talking about. What tracts that my grandmother wrote? I knew nothing about any of this, and the confusion on my face revealed my ignorance.

"You don't know that your grandmother writes for an abolitionist newspaper published in Boston, do you?"

Miss Amanda looked as if she'd let the cat out of the bag, and she had. "Your grandmother writes articles for publications in Boston and in other cities. She writes under the pen name of 'Liberty Belle.' I probably shouldn't have said anything, but I assumed you must know about your grandmother's activities. She writes often for *The Liberator*, but she writes for other abolitionist publications, too. She is a great woman."

I knew my grandmother had grown up and gone to school in Boston. Of course I knew about her strong anti-slavery views. She was a Quaker. But I had no idea she wrote articles that were published and read all over the country. She had kept this secret from me, and I knew there was a reason she had kept her secret. I suspected she did not want anyone in Burley to know that she was Liberty Belle. Slavery was legal in Maryland, and Gram had a position in our town as Grandpa Doc's wife. She made no secret of her views, but I doubted anyone in our town suspected that she was a nationally known writer. And Gram did not want anybody to know. Her secret life was safe with me, but I was curious and wanted to read what she had written.

Miss Amanda went to another room and returned with a clipping from a newspaper in her hand. "Your grandmother wrote this. I save each and every one of her articles." I took the piece of the newspaper she handed me and read what my dear Gram had written:

FREEDOM LIVES

Freedom lives in the hearts of all men and women everywhere. No matter what the color of their skin might be and no matter what their station in life, every human being yearns to be free. Every one of us must believe that we are the masters of our own fates, that nothing can contain or stifle our destinies. The natural human condition for all people is to be free. It is a God-given right. There is no substitute for freedom. It is like the air we breathe and the water we drink. It is the only true justice on God's earth. Be on notice, every person who tries to enslave another. Be on notice, you despots and tyrants, far and wide. Your day of reckoning will arrive. It may come while you walk the earth, or it may come at the Pearly Gates when Saint Peter asks you to answer for your sins. It is a sin to enslave another human being. If you have kept another human being as a slave, you have sinned. Every decent man and woman will strive for freedom, work for freedom, and live and die for freedom until it is achieved.

by Liberty Belle

This sounded exactly like what my Gram would write. It was what she believed. I was proud of her. I wasn't surprised that she would write these words or that she would publish her writings in a newspaper. What surprised me was that she had been able to keep her identity as Liberty Belle a secret for so long. I would help keep her secret. No one in Burley could know.

I knew that Gram was always writing letters. I knew she mailed many envelopes and packages to Boston. I had assumed this was all correspondence with her cousins and other relatives who lived in Massachusetts. I'd had no idea she was sending articles to be published in a newspaper. Things that had puzzled me about all the writing Gram did and all the things she put in the mail now became more understandable.

Miss Amanda was looking at me for a reaction to the article my Gram had written. There were many things I could say about Gram and her writing. I finally found my voice and looked at Amanda Mayfair. "She is really quite eloquent, isn't she?"

"Indeed she is. Indeed she is." Miss Amanda was obviously a great admirer of Liberty Belle.

At that moment, Grandpa Doc walked into the kitchen. He looked so tired, and his face was an unhealthy shade of gray. He had been awake all night taking care of Solomon and hadn't had any sleep. "I have good news, Louisa. Solomon is going to live. He's not going to lose his leg, and with lots of hard work, I think he will be able to walk again."

I was shocked, as I'd not known Solomon was in danger of losing his leg, let alone his life. I had not realized there was a chance he wouldn't walk again. I ran to Grandpa Doc and threw myself into his arms. I cried. I thanked him for saving Solomon. He patted me on the back and told me not to worry. He wanted to lighten the mood. "All right, Miss Amanda, how about serving me a plate of those buttermilk pancakes and some of that famous Mayfair Farms sugar-cured ham."

Miss Amanda was happy to change the subject, too. "Coming right up. How many pancakes do you want?"

I sat and waited while my grandfather ate his breakfast. I knew he wanted to lay his head down on a pillow and go to sleep, but I was too selfish to let him do that. I was desperate to see Solomon. "Grandpa Doc, will you take me to see Solomon? I think a visit from me would help him heal more quickly. I must tell him goodbye before we return to Burley. Please." I pleaded.

Grandpa Doc could see in my eyes and hear in my voice that this was important to me. "Of course you can visit him and tell him goodbye. But not today. He's in too much pain today. I will take you to see him tomorrow morning, before we leave to go home."

My carpet bag was packed, and we'd had our breakfast. The wagon and the horses my grandfather had borrowed were waiting outside the Mayfair's house. Darling, my grandfather's horse, was tied to the back of the wagon we would drive back to Burley. Ithaca would stay with the Mayfairs until her foot had healed. It was time to leave. My heart was heavy. I would be saying farewell to Solomon … probably forever. I doubted our paths would ever cross, at any time or place in the future. It was so difficult for me to accept that I would never see him again. My grandfather walked with me to the Mayfair's barn. There was a trap door under the hay in the floor of one of the horse stalls. Grandpa Doc led the horse to the next stall, pushed the hay aside with a rake, and opened the trap door. He warned me to be careful as I climbed down the narrow stairway. He followed me into the cellar of the barn and led me to a tiny room where Solomon lay on a cot.

When Solomon looked up and saw me, he smiled a big smile. I knelt down beside the cot and took his hand. I leaned in close to speak to him. "How is your leg? Do you have a lot of pain?"

"I'd like to say I don't have no pain, but the truth is, I've got a heap a pain. But Grandpa Doc tells me I'll be fine. It'll take a long time, but I'll walk again. I will give it my best try."

"You always give everything your best try, Solomon." I was struggling not to allow my voice to tremble. "I am going to miss you terribly, but I am very happy that you will soon be a free man. You will have a new family and a new life. You are incredibly smart, and you will be able to get a good education in Philadelphia."

"I'll be forever thankful for your teachin' me to read

and write. I'd never hope to go to a decent school if you hadn't helped me learn."

"You really taught yourself, Solomon. You know that. I was just there to provide you with the books and the paper and pens you needed." My grandfather was standing by the door to Solomon's room, and he gave me a sign that it was time to leave. "I have to go now. I will never forget you."

"I'll never forget you, Louisa. I'll always remember you in my prayers, and I wish for you to have a happy life. You're a real special person."

"You are a special person, too, Solomon. Very special." I squeezed his hand, and he squeezed mine back. The tears started to roll down my cheeks. I could see a tear in the corner of Solomon's eye. I leaned over and hugged my friend goodbye. Then I ran out of the room and began to sob. I hoped Solomon couldn't hear me crying.

My grandfather closed the door to Solomon's room. "Come along now, Louisa. Solomon is going to be fine. He will recover, and he will be walking again soon. In a few weeks, he will be on his way to Philadelphia. The Mayfairs are good people and will take care of him. They will be sure he travels safely to freedom." I knew all of the things my grandfather was saying were true. I knew Solomon would be safe and would finally be free. That wasn't why I was crying. I was sad because I was saying goodbye to someone I cared about, someone I had dearly loved for a long time. It was a like a death. From this day forward, Solomon would be dead to me.

My grandfather led me by the hand to the back of the barn's basement. He said, "Here, let me show you." There was a rack of farm implements hanging on the wall. As he lifted the hoe off the rack, part of the wall swung sideways. A small opening appeared, and I could see a tunnel that stretched out ahead for a long way. "Solomon and many other slaves will, in the future, pass through this hidden doorway. Many others have already traveled this route and found their way to a thick woods where they have met with friends of freedom, our conductors on the Underground Railroad. They are transported out of the hell that is slavery. This is their escape route. This is their portal to the future."

I nodded, and when Grandpa Doc put the hoe back on the rack, the wall silently and seamlessly closed. One would never know a doorway was there. I knew Solomon would recover because I trusted my grandfather. I knew Solomon would make it to Philadelphia because I trusted the Mayfairs and had seen for myself that they had an excellent way to hide him and to move him. I appreciated all of this.

We climbed back up the narrow stairway. My grandfather put the hay over the trap door and returned the horse to its stall. We walked from the barn to the wagon. The Mayfairs were waiting there to tell us goodbye. I hugged Miss Amanda and thanked her for everything.

"We will take good care of Solomon, and I will send you a letter when he leaves us to make his way to Philadelphia."

I climbed up onto the seat of the wagon next to my grandfather. He took the reins, and the horses began to move. I waved to the Mayfairs. I said a silent goodbye to Solomon. My heart was breaking. Life should not be this way. I should not have to say goodbye forever to a friend. I wondered if I would ever be the same again after this trip to Georgetown, Delaware.

My grandfather spoke. "We know you taught Solomon to read and write. We always knew you were meeting him and teaching him in secret. We were proud of you for your commitment and your courage. You gave him the tools he needs to have a successful future life as a free man. You gave him the confidence to break the bonds of slavery. You can always be proud of the gift you gave to Solomon." He looked at me and saw my tears were flowing again. "I know this is hard for you, Louisa. Life often presents us with difficult choices. Would you choose to have Solomon stay behind and remain a slave on the plantation?"

"Of course not." I snuffled out the words.

"So, when you are feeling sad that your friend has moved away and on to a better life, you must remind yourself of exactly that ... that it is a better life for him. You must remind yourself of the important role you have played in providing him with that better life."

I knew what Grandpa Doc was trying to say to me, but all of his wise words and all of his truth could not take away from my heart the sting of parting.

CHAPTER TEN

Changing Seasons

3-8-1-14-7-9-14-7 19-5-1-19-15-14-19

M y life *was forever changed after making the* trip to Georgetown and saying farewell to Solomon. My mother, my grandparents, and even my brother noticed that I was much quieter than usual. Even Cranky knew I was sad. She gave me extra affection and tried to cheer me. I worked hard in the gardens, and my mother, Gram, Sally, and I all worked in the kitchen to preserve the bounty of the end-of-the-summer harvest. Canning food in glass jars was a new way to keep food from spoiling over the winter months. Gram had ordered jars and lids and rubber rings from a store in New York, and we were especially careful to follow all of the directions about how to use this new method to preserve our food.

We canned tomatoes, green beans, lima beans, corn, peaches, pears, plums, and pickles. It was a hectic and busy end to the summer, with all the work we had to do picking and canning. I thought if I had to peel another tomato or stuff another one into another jar, I would scream. We made all kinds of jams and jellies and preserved them in small glass containers sealed with paraffin. We still dried some of our food, as we have always done. My grandfather likes dried tomatoes and dried fruits. We put the potatoes and onions and apples down into barrels filled with straw and stored them in our cellar. We made apple cider and apple cider vinegar. It had been an abundant harvest, and I was happy to know that we would eat well all winter long.

We moved some people along the Underground Railroad at the end of the summer. I did not see many of them, as they arrived and left under the cover of darkness. I think my family was trying to protect me because of the difficulties we had encountered on the mission to Georgetown. It made me feel better to stay busy. I wanted to be useful, and my mother did allow me to help her put the quilts on the line. We did a lot of subterfuge, and she and I laughed together when we were putting quilts on the line that meant nothing. We put them there to fool the slave hunters and to fool Ava.

School would be starting soon, and I was glad of that. I loved learning, and I liked to go to school. I would see some friends again that I hadn't seen all summer. I looked forward to the fall and to the cooler weather.

My brother Joseph would be leaving in a few days to attend school in Washington, D.C. He'd been cooped up inside for most of the summer with his tutor, who was preparing him for the work he would be doing at his new school. Joseph had been out of sorts about the fact that he'd had to study all summer, and he was mad at me because I'd been the one to have the adventures and the fun. He'd not been allowed to tell Solomon goodbye, and that had made him angry with our mother and our grandparents. He had new clothes to wear, and he thought he looked silly in the city clothes and the uniform his school required. He complained all the time and was always in a grouchy mood.

He knew he had to work hard at his studies in order to be prepared for his new school. He was excited about living with our cousins in the nation's capital, but he was also scared. He tried not to let anybody know he was scared, and he would never have admitted to me that he was anything but brave and confident. But I could tell he was worried about leaving home and worried about whether or not he would be able keep up with the other students at the private academy. All of our cousins went to the Quaker school. It wasn't like he wouldn't know anybody, but it was a big change for him and for all of us. I would miss him, too, but I knew I would see him again at Christmas and all next summer. It wasn't like it had been with Solomon … saying goodbye forever.

Grandpa Doc was going to drive Joseph in the carriage to Washington, D.C. and help him settle in with my Aunt Margaret and Uncle Angus. Grandpa Doc would go with Joseph for his first day of school. It was important to my family that Joseph have the best possible education. My grandfather would be gone for almost a week. He never left town for more than a day or two at a time because he was the only doctor in town. Taking Joseph to school was important to him, and Grandpa Doc wanted to be sure everything went smoothly for his grandson. I was a little envious that Joseph was getting so much attention and that everyone cared so much about his education. At the same time, I was glad I didn't have to leave home to go to school. I was at the head of my class at the grammar school in Burley, and that suited me just fine.

One Saturday morning, when I went out in my backyard to play with Cranky, I looked across Crooked Creek and saw a red quilt on our neighbor's clothesline. I knew this meant danger. It meant no slaves were to be moved. There was to be no activity on the Underground Railroad. I ran inside to tell my mother. She would know what to do and would be able to find out what was happening.

My mother stood on the bank of Crooked Creek for a long time and looked at the red quilt on the clothesline across the water. I know she had seen a red quilt on the line from time to time in the past, but she seemed especially worried by this sign today. "What's wrong,

Mama? I know this quilt signal means danger. What are we going to do?"

"I don't know, Louisa. The danger signal means I am not supposed to go to the house across the creek. It means I must stay away. Something is very wrong, and I cannot do anything to find out what it is. My instinct is to go across the creek to find out what's happening, but the red quilt on the line is the code for ... 'don't do anything.'"

"May I take my rowing boat across the creek and try to find out what's going on?"

"I'm not going to put you at risk again. We are all still suffering from the worry and the guilt because we asked you to drive Solomon to Georgetown alone in the pony cart. We were desperate, but we should never have allowed you to take on that mission. I almost lost you, and I will never forgive myself for that."

My grandfather had left with Joseph the day before to travel to Washington, D.C. I knew my mother wished she could talk with Grandpa Doc about what to do regarding the red quilt. She saddled up her horse, and I saddled up my pony. We rode into town and went to visit Gram. She wasn't expecting us for lunch, but she was delighted to see us. As usual, she had plenty of food. At Gram's house, we always eat lunch in the dining room, and today Celia, Gram's cook, served us delicious plates of chicken salad with sliced tomatoes. There were freshly baked hot rolls with butter and raspberry jam. I loved my Gram's chicken salad and her raspberry jam. We drank iced tea and had sponge cake with chocolate icing for dessert. It was a special treat to eat lunch with Gram.

My mother waited until the table had been cleared before she brought up the subject of the red quilt. "There was a red signal across the creek from the farm today. Of course, I'm worried about what it means. If Grandpa Doc were here, he would be able to find out what's wrong, but he isn't here. And he won't be here for several days. I'm wondering if I should go over there and try to find out what's happening. Have you heard anything?"

"I have heard that a family was supposed to be moved the day before yesterday, but they didn't arrive as scheduled. They were to come by water and go directly from the creek to the widow's house. The plan was to move them the rest of the way by land, to Delaware and north from there. I am worried something has gone wrong with that plan. Maybe one of the members of the family became ill. As you know, we have been keeping our eyes out for the snoopy girl Ava, and I think we have succeeded in cutting off her supply of information about the Underground Railroad. But I don't know what's wrong at the house across the creek from you. It was supposed to be a routine operation … if anything we do can be considered to be routine. There were no infants or small children in the family. It was supposed to be four people, and they were all said to be healthy enough to walk on their own. At least, that is what we were expecting, and that's why we decided to transport them to Delaware and points north by land. Obviously, something has gone wrong, but I don't know what's happened. As you say, Grandpa Doc might be able to find out, if he were here, but he's not here and won't be back until next week."

I wanted to help, so I spoke up. "I can take my boat across the creek to see if I can find out anything."

"No!" My Gram had felt especially guilty about what had happened to me on the trip to Georgetown. She didn't want me doing anything more that was the least bit dangerous. "I will try to find out something on my own. Grandpa Doc and I agreed we were not going to put you at risk any more until you are older."

"I want to help. I'm not afraid. You are all making more out of how hard the trip to Georgetown was on me than it really was. The worst thing that happened on that trip was saying goodbye to Solomon, not any of the other difficulties."

"Let me try to find out something, and then we will talk again. I will bring lunch to the farm tomorrow, and I might stay for dinner. Depending on what I am able to learn between now and then, I may want to stay at Elderberry Farm overnight. We will have to see." My Gram was always so confident and certain about what she was going to do. I wondered if I would ever be as sure of anything.

My mother and I rode our horses back to the farm. We were shocked to see that there were now two red quilts on the clothesline of the house across the creek. I'd never heard of two red quilts being put out at one time. "What does it mean when there are two red quilts on the line?"

My mother said that this sign was new to her, too. "I've never seen that particular signal before, and I can only guess that the danger has increased for some reason. What else could it possibly mean? It's not part of our regular code, but it is obviously meant to send a strong message. I will tell you that a widow owns the farm over there. She's a free Negro woman who lives by herself. She owns her farm. Her husband, who was also a free Negro, died years ago. She never remarried after her husband died. She lives a quiet life and she's never had any children. She doesn't go out much. She doesn't often hide slaves in her own house. She is mostly the person who signals to me and conveys my signals to others. The location of her farm is such that her back yard and her quilts can be seen by walkers and boaters who go up and down Crooked Creek and travel around on other inlets and small waterways. Because her farm is located on a point of land that sticks out into the water, her clothesline can also be seen by large ships that come up into some of the ocean coves. In good weather, her fence can be seen from some places all the way out at sea. It's the location that makes her farm so important. The ships in the coves know from her signals when it is safe to approach to pick up or drop off a freedom traveler and when it isn't safe. Her sign may not be for me at all. It may be that the widow hopes a ship at sea will take heed of the two red quilts."

CHAPTER ELEVEN

Nothing Is Perfect

14-15-20-8-9-14-7   9-19   16-5-18-6-5-3-20

My Gram arrived the next day in her one-horse carriage. She brought a roasted turkey breast in a picnic basket. She had soft rolls, her special salad dressing, greens, sliced tomatoes, and all the fixings for a delicious turkey sandwich. She brought a cold carrot salad that was sweet and sour, dressed with cider vinegar and a little bit of molasses. She had little pots of vanilla custard for dessert. Celia had made the custard, and I knew it would be delicious. My mother brought out a pitcher of lemonade. It was a beautiful early September day, and we ate on the table in the yard. Gram didn't wait for us to finish eating before she gave us the news.

"The family that was supposed to arrive by boat two days ago ...." She paused, not knowing quite how to break the bad news to us. "They didn't make it. Their boat sank. It was an old fishing boat, a dory, and should not have been on the water at all. When people are desperate, they do desperate things, things that aren't safe. The dory wasn't safe. The family was coming from North Carolina. They made it to the mouth of the Chesapeake Bay on foot and decided to commandeer the old fishing boat. They sailed north along the coast of the Eastern Shore of Virginia and made it across the Maryland State line. The family of four thought their boat could make it to Burley, but they only made it to Assateague Island beach where the boat sank. They weren't familiar with the area, and they were lost. They made it ashore on the island and then assumed they could walk to their meeting place in Burley. But of course they couldn't. They were on an island, and none of them could swim. They should have been with a guide, but they thought they could do it on their own. It was two brothers and their sons, four men traveling together."

"Why didn't they split them up? It's always so much more difficult to move a group of people." My mother knew how things were supposed to work when we moved people along their journeys to freedom.

"The men were going to be separated. They were to be sold on the courthouse steps, someplace in North Carolina. Slaves endure beatings, hard labor, starvation, and mistreatment of all kinds. They suffer through all of these things, but what pushes them to the breaking point is when the master threatens to separate them from each other. This is when family members, faced with being sold off and sent to different farms or plantations or even states, often make the decision to try to escape. That was the case with this family."

"I can understand that. Breaking families apart is the cruelest thing a slave owner can do."

"Also, one of the sons is slow, and his father couldn't leave him behind or allow him to try to escape on his own. The worse news is that two of the four have been captured by slave hunters. We don't know where they've been taken, and we may never know. They may have been sent back where they came from. They may have been taken to prison. They may be hostages in the home of a slave catcher or another slave holder, waiting to be resold to another plantation. Or, something worse may have happened to them." Gram stopped talking, and then she sighed. She looked worried. "We also don't know what has happened to the two men who were not caught. Those two need help to reach the next stop on their journey, but we can't find them to tell them where to go. I'm worried that the slave hunters have gone to the widow's house. The slave hunters might be staying there or are keeping a watch on her farm. Because she's a Negro woman, they would naturally assume she is helping slaves escape."

"One of us needs to go over there and see what's going on. But the red quilts on the line mean to stay away …

that there is danger. I don't know what to do." My mother was anxious to help but didn't know how.

Gram knew what she intended to do. "I'm going to go over there. I don't want you or Louisa to go anywhere near that house. I'm an old woman. I'm the doctor's wife. I will say I've heard she had an illness in the household and that's why I've turned up on her doorstep. I will find out what is going on."

Hopefully the two men who'd not been captured yet were still alive. "We need to find these men. Where could they be? I hope they didn't drown trying to get across the bay from Assateague Island." I was difficult for me to accept that the network of moving slaves to freedom hadn't worked this time. "Is there nothing we can do about the two who were caught?"

"We can't do anything about the two who've been captured. We don't know what's happened to them or where they are. This family group tried to hurry their journey and didn't wait for the conductor to bring them. They were desperate and took the fishing boat." My Gram could see that I was disturbed by the news that two escaping slaves might have been returned to captivity or worse. "We can't save them all, Louisa. We do what we can. Sometimes we can't help them — especially when they take things into their own hands and especially when they act independently in unfamiliar territory. I'm not casting any blame here. I understand that they were impatient and frightened and didn't want to wait. They thought they could do it on their own, but they couldn't.

This has happened before, and it will happen again. And, sometimes, even when the people we are trying to save do everything we tell them to do, they are captured anyway. It isn't a perfect practice, and sometimes we fail. I hate to fail. We do everything to try to be sure we are successful, but we are not perfect. You have to learn to accept that there will be mistakes and failures even when we have done everything right." Gram reached over and gave me a reassuring pat on my hand.

"I'm going to be on my way now. It takes so much longer to go by land." Gram gave my mother the leftover food for us to have for supper and gathered up the rest of the picnic things and returned them to her basket. "I will try to stop on my way back to let you know what I've discovered."

Gram was driving her one-horse cart to the widow lady's house. If I'd gone by water, I would have taken my rowing boat down and across Crooked Creek. It would have taken no time at all to go by water. My Gram had to travel there by land, and that meant going the long way around on the road to get to the bridge that crossed the creek. I hoped she wasn't putting herself in danger by going to the house with the red quilts on the line.

My mother and I didn't want to go to bed until my grandmother returned from her mission. As the minutes and then the hours passed, I could see my mother becoming more and more worried. Where was Gram? Why had she not returned from the widow's house? We had thought we would wait up for Gram, but we finally decided to go to bed. I knew my mother wouldn't be able to go to sleep until Gram returned, and I wondered if I would be able to fall asleep. I needn't have worried, as Cranky and I fell asleep the minute I put my head down on the pillow.

I was awakened by loud knocking at the front door of our farmhouse. When I reached the upstairs hall, my mother was racing down the steps to see who was making such a racket in the middle of the night. In her hand she held a lantern to light her way. I hoped it would be my Gram returning, but I knew she wouldn't come to the front door. And she wouldn't have to knock.

Three rough men were at the door, and they looked mean. One held a lantern and a whip. I stayed at the top of the stairs, but I was ready to rush down to the front hall to help protect my mother if she needed me. The men were shouting at her. "We know you have two runaway slaves here. We know your mother brought them to your farm from across the creek, and you are hiding them."

"I have no idea what you are talking about. There are no slaves here … either hiding or otherwise. My mother isn't here either. As far as I know she is at her own house in Burley, fast asleep. Everyone should be fast asleep at this time of the night. You can search my house, and you are welcome to search my farm. But I will tell you ahead of time that you are wasting your time. There is no one here at this house except my daughter and myself."

My mother would have liked to block their way, but the men pushed into the house. Mama walked deliberately to the cupboard beside the door and picked up her shotgun, her box of shot, her wadding, and her powder horn. Everybody who lives on a farm outside of town keeps a shotgun by the door of the house. The gun is there mostly to use to keep the wolves away, but in this case, the wolves had two legs and were more menacing than the four-legged kind. My mother made a big production of stacking the box of shot and her wadding on the table by the front door. She stood in the middle of the front hall with her feet firmly planted on the floor, while she expertly and dramatically loaded the double-barrel muzzle-loader. She was ready. I knew she would never fire the gun at a person … even at these terrible people, but I smiled to myself that she was putting on such a good show. These scruffy men couldn't know for sure whether or not my mother would put buckshot in their britches.

The men searched the first floor, and then they stomped up the stairs to search the second floor. They didn't even look at me when they rudely pushed past me to go through our bedrooms. I found myself becoming awfully angry that they thought they could force their way into our home and look in closets and under beds at will. There was something very wrong about what they were doing. But my mother had said they were welcome to search. I guess she had to be pretty certain they wouldn't find anything.

She stood with her back to the front door, holding the shotgun, as they made their way through every room of our house. They boldly bragged that they'd already searched the barns and other out buildings. That sounded like trespassing to me. They were angry that they hadn't found anything. "You think you have outsmarted us this time, and you may have. But we will be back. We will be back again and again until we find our property, the property that is rightfully ours. Be on notice that we will bring you to justice for stealing from slave owners. You are hiding what rightfully belongs to them. You are breaking the law. You are the thief. We will get you one day, and you will pay the price."

Finally they left, and I ran down the stairs and threw myself into my mother's arms. I had been so afraid something would happen to her. I started to cry. She held me tightly. After a few minutes, she gently let me go. She put her muzzle-loader and the shot, the wadding, and the powder horn away in the cupboard by the door. I could see she was shaken, but she was more angry than frightened. "Now we have to figure out where Gram is hiding and where she's hidden the slaves. I think I know, but I don't want to go after her for fear the slave hunters are watching the house. She's smart about things like this, and she's had lots of experience. I expect she will watch the house until these rude slave hunters have gone away. Then she will let us know where she is and what we need to do."

I was too angry and too worried to go back to sleep now. My mother and I went into the kitchen, and she began to warm up milk on the stove to make hot cocoa for us to drink. She got cups down from the cupboard and brought some leftover cake from the pantry. We were going to have a vigil. I didn't think I could possibly sleep, but after I'd finished my cup of cocoa and a piece of cake, I fell sound asleep with my head on the table.

CHAPTER TWELVE

Saving Two for Freedom

19-1-22-9-14-7   20-23-15   6-15-18   6-18-5-5-4-15-13

I t was noon the next day when Sally came to the house. She hurried in the back door where my mother and I were sewing pieces of cloth together for quilt tops. I was pretty good at putting together the scraps of fabric, but my mother was still in charge of designing the patterns. "The slave hunters have just left the farm. I had to delay coming to tell you until they were gone. The two slaves are hiding in the ice house. Mrs. Doc and I put them there last night." Sally gave us the news we'd been waiting to hear.

The ice house was where we kept our perishable food. The small shed was very cold inside and had two wells of water on either side of a central brick walkway. The well on one side was deep, and that was where we stored large crocks and tall milk jugs. The well on the other side of the walkway was shallow, and we kept smaller bowls and containers of food cold on that side. The wells were lined with bricks and stones and cement, and both were filled with very cold water and blocks of ice. Our workmen cut big blocks of ice from the frozen ponds in the winter and put them in the wells inside the ice house. We usually were able to make our ice last through the spring and summer, until the cold weather came again. If we ran out of ice, we could buy ice in town. Buying ice was expensive so we tried not to buy any. Besides keeping the milk, and other things that might spoil, in the ice house, in the summer we chipped ice away from the huge blocks. We used the ice chips and chunks in glasses of lemonade and iced tea and to make ice cream. The ice house is an important place on our farm, and on every farm.

Our ice house has a special secret hiding place in it. It is a tiny space, just big enough for one person to stand up in. It is perfectly concealed in the brick wall at the end of the walkway that divides the two wells of cold water. Gram and Sally had somehow managed to get both of the escaped slaves into the space to hide them from the slave hunters. I could only imagine how chilled and cramped they must be if they had been in there all night. It was September, so most of the ice from the winter before had melted by now, but it would still have been terribly uncomfortable to be scrunched for hours into that small, cold hiding place. It would have been especially unpleasant for two people to be hidden in a space intended for only one.

The original plan and the schedule that had been set up to transport these men to freedom had completely fallen apart. Four men had begun the journey, and there were only two left to continue. They were days late in arriving, and new plans had to be put in place to safely move them. They said they wanted to go to Canada, and that was a much more complicated route to arrange. Getting them to Philadelphia would be difficult enough. I knew if anybody could figure out what to do, it would be my mother and my grandmother.

At this moment, we had to get the two men out of the ice house and to some place warm. Our house and farm buildings didn't really have many places to hide escaping slaves. We were more of a communications hub than a place for hiding people. We hung quilts on the line and provided transportation … by land and water.

Sally was worried about these two men because the younger one was feeble-minded. "He cries all the time and keeps saying he wants his father. His father was captured by slave hunters, and no one has any idea where the father is now. The older man is his uncle, and he's done everything he can to comfort his nephew who is so distraught. The four men who started this journey were two brothers, and each of them brought along his son. One of the brothers and one of the younger men were caught. The feeble-minded young man's father and the uncle's son were both captured. The young man's crying is a problem because it is necessary for the two to stay completely quiet wherever they are hiding. This young man seems to be very sweet, but he doesn't understand why he has to be silent. We have tried to explain it to him, but he just cries and cries. Sometimes his wailing is so loud. It may be a few days before Mrs. Doc is able to arrange to move these men, and we have to find a place for the younger one where no one will hear him crying."

I was listening to Sally describe the two slaves who were trying to make their journey to freedom, and I felt so sorry for the poor young man who had the mind and emotions of a little boy. He couldn't understand what had happened to his father, and he missed his father, in the way a small child quite naturally would miss a parent. I could see this was a problem for many reasons. The slave hunters were looking everywhere, and they would be watching our farm closely.

I could tell my mother was worried when she said, "I need to talk to Gram. These two can't stay in the ice house, and we don't have a good place to hide them here at Elderberry Farm. The slave hunters say they've already searched all the outbuildings. For now, we will hide them in the quilting barn."

My mother helped Sally remove the bricks that obscured the tiny hiding place in the ice house, and we freed the two slaves from the dampness. They were stiff and sore from being kept in such a confining space, and they were happy to get out of the cold shed. Mama gave instructions to Sally. "Give these two some food and hot soup and hide them in the cupboard in the quilting barn. We have to take that chance, but they can't stay there for more than a few hours."

I wanted to help and had an idea that might work to soothe the troubled young man. We saddled up our horses to ride into town to talk to Gram. She must have driven her cart back to her house in town last night after leaving the two slaves at our ice house. She would tell us what had happened and what she was planning for their journey. Because of the young man's loud crying, he and his uncle could not stay at Gram's. She couldn't keep the escaping slaves at her house in town because there were always too many people around. The doctor's house was a favorite gathering place for people to get the news and to come when they were sick or in trouble. I knew Grandpa Doc and Gram smuggled slaves through their house, but it always happened at night and happened silently. I was sure the women could handle this, but we all wished Grandpa Doc was available. He always had good ideas about how to solve a problem.

My Gram was working at her writing desk when we arrived. She was glad to see us, and I could tell she was eager to share what had happened after she'd left our house the day before. She looked tired but energized. I could see she was working on a plan.

"Come in and let me tell you about my adventure. I rode my horse cart over to the widow's house. Remember, we must not mention any names. I knocked and knocked, and it was a long time before she came to the door. She was terrified, but when she saw me, she opened the door and let me come inside. She said the two Negroes had come to her back door the night before last. She knew her house was being closely watched, so she told them to hide in the nearby cornfield. She took food and water to them in the field. She was frightened, not so much for herself, but for the two men. She said to me that she is an old woman and doesn't really care what happens to her. But she was unusually worried about this pair. She said the younger one of the two men was feeble-minded and cried all the time. The older man, the boy's uncle, explained that the young man's father had been captured by the slave hunters, and the boy-man was suffering from missing his father. The widow couldn't hide the two inside. She told them her house was being watched, and the slave catchers could come at any moment and search. The wailing of the younger slave would have given them away in no time. So she sent them to the corn field. It's difficult to find someone in a corn field without a dog. She just had to hope and pray that the slave hunters did not have dogs. In case the people who were hunting them did have dogs, they needed to keep moving around in circles. If they walked around in circles, the scent would throw off the dogs who would chase themselves around in circles. But the men were exhausted, and they were going to have to sleep. The widow told the escaping slaves to dig a trench and cover themselves up with mud when they wanted to go to sleep. If they covered themselves up with dirt, the dirt would mask their human scent. To the dogs, they would smell like dirt, and they could sleep. The widow was panicked. She didn't think she could keep them hidden in the cornfield for another day."

"How did you get them back to our farm?" I had to know.

"I knew I couldn't take them into town. When he was awake, the feeble-minded boy's crying was so loud. Everyone in Burley would hear him. The only place I could think of taking them was to your ice house. They were covered with mud and manure from sleeping in a trench in the corn field and covering themselves up with dirt. I told them to wash off in the creek. They finally got clean enough for me to let them into my little buggy. I put a blanket over the two of them, and it was a tight squeeze in that buggy, let me tell you. The young man who cried all the time thought the ride was exciting and stopped crying while we were going fast enough. Whenever we would slow down or stop, though, he would begin to cry again. I thought we would never make it to your ice house. I told them what they had to do. I woke Sally, and we moved the bricks to allow them to get into the hiding place. They didn't really both fit in there, but I told them it was a matter of life and death. I was so afraid the slave hunters would search your ice house and hear the boy crying. I told the uncle he had to keep his nephew quiet, but there was little he or anyone could do about that."

"You know they want to go to Canada." My mother was certain Gram knew this, but she was just reminding her. "They don't want to go to Philadelphia because of the boy. Because of his feeblemindedness, the uncle is afraid he will be too easily identified as an escaped slave. If he is found in Philadelphia, slave hunters can return him to his plantation and his former masters. The Slave Act of 1850 made that legal. If they can make it to Canada, he can never be caught and returned to slavery. So, it makes sense that the boy and his uncle should try to go to Canada. Most of the time we don't try to get our Underground Railroad passengers that far, but this time, it seems like it is worth the effort … and really quite necessary."

"That's why this journey has become so complicated. We are making arrangements to get them to Canada. We are trying to get them out of the United States without having them stop in Philadelphia or anyplace in this country." Gram lowered her voice. She didn't want Ava or whatever spy might be listening in on our plans to hear what she had to say. "We are going to put them onto a clipper ship that is sailing directly to Nova Scotia. At least we are trying to arrange for this type of transport. It will be a British ship, not an American ship. Once the two are aboard the British ship, they will be safe. But making all these arrangements at the last minute has been almost impossible." Gram never said the word impossible, and I worried when I heard her say it now.

"I've found a place to hide them in a barn on a dairy farm. The farm is north of here. The problem is the boy's crying. It seems there is no comfort for the poor lad.

He misses his father and can't understand what has happened to him. He will probably never see his father again. If the boy cries too much or is too loud with his crying, the dairy farmer won't keep him in his barn. And I can't blame him for that."

I spoke up. "I have an idea, Gram, an idea that might help the sad boy stop crying. I've noticed something about Morley Colbert, the boy who lives down the street from you, the one who is also very slow. When I see him in town and I have Cranky with me, it's almost as if Morley becomes a different person. He kneels down and pets Cranky. He will even get down on his hands and knees and talk to her. He puts his face in her fuzzy white hair and loves to let her lick his face. When I thought about how much Morley loves Cranky, I was wondering if maybe we should try letting the feebleminded boy spend some time with Cranky. He might find some comfort with her, and he might stop crying if he has her close by. What do you think?"

"I think it's a first-rate idea, and I wish I had thought of it. It is the best suggestion I have heard so far, and it is certainly worth a try. None of our great schemes with dairy barns and clipper ships and Nova Scotia will amount to a hill of beans if we can't get the child to stop his howling." Gram loved my idea.

Mama hugged me, and we left Gram's house to get back on our horses. The sooner we got the two slaves out of the cupboard in the quilting barn the better. The sooner we introduced Cranky to the feebleminded boy, the better. We were on our way. That evening, someone would arrive at our farm with a hay wagon, and hopefully, we would send the two slaves on to their next destination.

It was dark when we arrived back at the farm. Cranky and I ran to the quilting barn. Mama let the slaves out of their hiding place. Cranky immediately ran to the young man, and she jumped up into his arms. It was as if she instinctively knew what she was supposed to do, and she did it. She licked the boy's face, and he laughed. The young man and the little white dog instantly formed a bond, and it seemed as if things were going to be all right.

The hay wagon arrived soon after, and the two slaves and Cranky climbed aboard and covered themselves with hay. The driver of the hay wagon would drive north and hand the two men over to the dairy farmer who would keep them hidden. When the time was right, a conductor for the Underground Railway would arrange for the two to make it safely to the clipper ship bound for Nova Scotia. The man who drove the hay wagon promised that, when the two slaves had moved on to the next stage of their journey, he would bring Cranky back to me.

I would miss Cranky while she was on her mission, but she was the best of dogs. She always calmed me when I was upset. I knew she wouldn't let me down. I loved her so much. She had just become a mini-conductor on the Underground Railroad. I was proud of her and knew she would soon be home and sleeping on my bed again.

It was about an hour's ride to the dairy farm, their next station on the Underground Railroad, and I had a feeling it was going to work out for these two. Nova Scotia was in their future. The young man would always struggle, and he would never stop missing his father. But we had given him the chance to live in freedom. Who knew what opportunities might open up for the feeble-minded boy? I would sleep well tonight, even without my beloved fluffy dog.

CHAPTER THIRTEEN

School Begins Again

19-3-8-15-15-12   2-5-7-9-14-19   1-7-1-9-14

ecause many crops in our part of the world are harvested in late summer, school didn't begin in Burley until the middle of September. It was a farm community, and children were needed to get the sheaves from the fields into the barn and to provide extra labor to help with threshing. Slaves and hired hands mostly harvested the cotton, but on some farms, children also did this work. Small hands are good at plucking the cotton bolls from the plants. Children were essential to the farm economy of the Mid-Atlantic. The school calendar was scheduled around the work that families had to do to survive.

It had been a magical summer for me, and I would

never be the same person again. I felt years older. But I was excited to be going back to school because I couldn't wait to immerse myself in the new subjects I hoped to study. My book learning always came first, but I also wanted to continue to participate in the activities of the Underground Railroad. I knew the quilt code by heart now, backwards and forwards. I could take over when my mother wasn't able to put the quilts on the line. My self-confidence had grown because I felt I was doing something important, something vital to the cause of freedom.

When I went to my grandparents' house after school one day, Gram had left a letter propped up on the kitchen table with my milk and cookies. The letter was addressed to me, and the return address indicated that it was from Georgetown, Delaware, from Amanda Mayfair. I tore the letter open even before I reached for the first delicious cookie. I was hoping against hope there would be news of Solomon. It had been weeks since I'd left him in the basement of the Mayfair's barn. Amanda had promised she would write to me when Solomon left her house to continue his journey to Philadelphia. The letter was two pages long, and I read it with great eagerness.

Most of the letter was just news about what was happening on their farm. Miss Amanda wrote about an especially good crop of apples from their orchard, the applesauce she had made, and the apple cider vinegar that had turned out so well. She told me how many quart jars of vegetables she had canned. I was happy to hear all of this, but I was mostly looking for information about what had happened to Solomon. Finally, in the last paragraph of her letter, Miss Amanda wrote:

Farmer George and I attended an excellent concert at the Georgetown Methodist Church last weekend. The Songs were beautifully sung, and one mon in particular sang a breathtaking Solo. We enjoyed the music so much, and we were sorry when the concert ended. Later this year, we hope to attend another musical event in Philadelphia.

With Affection and True Regard,
Amanda Mayfair

This was the news I had been waiting for, good news about Solomon. Miss Amanda had written cryptically in case her letter was intercepted on its way to me, but she knew I would be able figure out what she was trying to say. My interpretation of her paragraph about the concert was that Solomon had left Mayfair Farm and was on his way to his new life in Philadelphia. Amanda had promised to let me know, and she had followed through with that promise. I so wanted to have more details about how Solomon's leg was healing and if he was walking again without any problems. But I was delighted to have this news that he had been well enough to continue his journey to freedom.

One Friday in October, when I rode my pony home to Elderberry Farm after school, I noticed there was a black quilt hanging on the widow's clothes line across Crooked Creek. I'd never seen a black quilt hanging anywhere before, but I knew it meant there had been a death and that help was needed. I rushed inside and found my mother and Sally at the kitchen table. Things were serious because they hardly noticed when I burst into the room.

"Mama, I saw the black quilt hanging on the widow's line. Do you know what's wrong? I know it means death, but who has died?"

"We don't know yet. The quilt just appeared on the line within the last hour. We are trying to decide what to do. We might ask you to go over there in your rowing boat. It's so much faster to reach the widow's farm by water."

"Please, let me go. I want to do it."

"We can't let you go until we know why someone's died. If there is a terrible plague or illness in the area, we can't let you go there."

"When will we know?"

"Grandpa Doc has someone heading over there now … to find out about the death. Grandpa Doc's helper will come to Elderberry Farm and let us know if it is safe to go to the widow's house. Hopefully we will know what is going on before dark."

But we hadn't heard anything by the time the sun went down. My mother and I went to bed as usual, but my mother woke me in the middle of the night. Gram had ridden her horse out to Elderberry Farm with news from Grandpa Doc. I knew things were serious because Gram had never before ridden her horse to our farm after dark. There was an emergency.

Grandpa Doc had sent someone to inquire about the death at the widow's farm on Crooked Creek. Gram had all the details about the young woman who had run away from her plantation in Virginia and made it as far as the widow's farm. "She was a relative, a distant cousin of some kind, of the widow. She was being brutally beaten on the plantation where she was a slave, and she was heavily pregnant with her child. She was able to escape and make it to the widow's house, but she was in labor when she arrived. The widow is a midwife and has birthed many babies, but she wasn't able to save the mother this time. The mother bled to death after giving birth, but the baby girl was full term and is reportedly healthy and thriving. The mother died yesterday. The widow is feeding the baby with goat's milk and a bottle contraption Grandpa Doc invented to feed babies whose mothers are unable to feed them." I knew that in a small town, it's often impossible to find a wet nurse to feed a motherless baby. Grandpa Doc has been working on perfecting his baby-feeding bottles for years. He uses a rubber tube and a small glass bottle, and he's had remarkable success keeping babies alive with his invention. He feeds these babies goat's milk. Grandpa Doc says the goat's milk agrees with newborns better than cow's milk does.

Gram continued. "We have to get the child out of the area as soon as possible. This baby is somebody special, although I don't know exactly why. The slave hunters are searching everywhere for the mother and child. They don't yet know that the mother has died."

"What can I do to help?"

"I'd not wanted you to help with any more Underground Railroad passengers ... after what you went through to save Solomon. But we may have to call on you this time. There is a very special conductor on the Railroad that people call Moses, and this mother and this baby are important to her. Moses knows the mother has died."

Gram continued. "Moses has other names. She was born Araminta "Minty" Ross. She escaped from slavery in Maryland, not far from Burley, and she now lives in Auburn, New York. When she escaped to freedom in 1849, she changed her name to Harriet Tubman. Although she is now free and would never have to risk returning to a slave state, she has chosen to return to Maryland, Delaware, and other places in the South many times, to escort members of her family and her friends to freedom. She's personally invested in seeing that this newborn baby escapes from slavery, and she is on her way from Upper New York State to Delaware to insure that the child makes it to freedom. There's a family up north someplace that is waiting to take the baby. Moses is already taking a huge risk by coming to Delaware, and she doesn't want to travel into Maryland. There is a bounty on her head. A reward of more than $12,000 has been offered for her capture. She says that, right now, it is too dangerous for her to travel south of the Mason and Dixon line. If we can get the baby across the line, Moses will take over to be sure the baby is safe and makes it the rest of the way to her new family. People say that Moses has no fear of anything. She says she would chose death over being a slave again. The rumor is that she carries a pistol in her pocket and is not afraid to use it. Although I have never met her, she has been a legend among agents of the Underground Railroad for at least a decade."

"I can take the baby over the Mason and Dixon line into Delaware. Please let me do that. I can take the baby to Moses." It had become important to me to be able to do my part in helping slaves gain their freedom. I had loved the work I'd done during the past summer, and I missed helping out. Just because I had to go to school didn't mean I couldn't participate as I had during the summer months. School work was easy for me. I learned quickly. My mother was thinking of having me put ahead a grade or two in school so I would be challenged. I easily had time and energy to help move slaves.

I knew there would be a big pow wow with my mother and my grandparents, before they would decide to allow me to help with this mission. I loved babies, and I especially wanted to be sure this baby made it to freedom. It was already a sad situation because the baby's mother had died in childbirth. Everybody was making an extra effort to be sure this baby would be able to continue the journey her mother was no longer able to make.

There was no one else in our area who could attempt the journey to Delaware. This trip was more dangerous because the slave hunters were out in force, trying to find the mother and the baby. If anyone realized that Moses was assisting in this mission, even more slave hunters would come to the area, looking for her because of the enormous reward being offered for her capture. The trip would be more dangerous because this time, the passenger who would be traveling on the Underground Railroad was a newborn infant.

The third factor that made this escape more difficult was the means of travel. I would have to walk to Delaware, and I would have to carry the baby all the way. We couldn't use a cart or a wagon of any kind. We could not use a horse or even take the chance of traveling on any roads, even on back roads. I would have to walk through the woods, not on any known paths and not near any farms.

All my life, I had played in the woods with my brother Joseph and with Solomon. I knew how to find my way through the brush and trees. Because I was a tomboy, my tracking skills would help me find my way. I was comfortable in the woods, but I would not have anyone to depend on except myself this time. I was familiar with some of the rough territory I would have to travel through. I knew my way around the woods near our farm and around Burley. In some places, I would have to cut my way through the thicket.

And, all the while I was walking in the woods, I would be carrying a newborn baby who was just a few days old. I would be responsible for taking care of the infant during the entire journey. Besides keeping her safe, I would have to be sure the baby was warm and clean and dry. I would have to feed the baby along the way. The risks were high, but I thought I could do it. My Gram was sure I could do it. My mother was not at all happy about my taking on this dangerous task, but she finally agreed.

The weather was growing colder by the day. Late in October, we could have snow flurries, even here on the Eastern Shore of Maryland. I would have to wear my warmest clothes, including a woolen cap, and I would wear several pairs of socks and my mother's winter boots lined with rabbit fur. The baby would be wrapped in the warmest baby bunting we could find. I would have to carry all of my own food as well as every ounce of the milk the baby would need.

All of these decisions and plans were made in a few hours. Everyone at my house was on edge. My mother was upset, but she was doing her best to pack everything I would require on the journey. Grandpa Doc was at the widow's house, seeing to the baby. There was so much going on around me, I didn't have time to be as nervous as I probably should have been.

CHAPTER FOURTEEN

The Impossible Journey

20-8-5 9-13-16-15-19-19-9-2-12-5 10-15-21-18-14-5-25

My family decided that I should set out on my journey the next night. I was familiar with the forests, the farms, and the bodies of water in the area close to my home. These were the well-known environs where I'd grown up and lived and played all my life. Gram thought I would be able to find my way in the dark in familiar territory. When the sun came up, she told me I would have to hide and rest. She wanted it to be daylight when I reached areas farther north where I would find myself in unknown terrain. I understood the plan. Years earlier, my mother had done this work on foot, and Gram had also walked to guide slaves to freedom. But neither one of them, even though they were experienced conductors on the Underground Railroad, had ever had a newborn infant as an Underground Railroad passenger.

My stomach was full of butterflies, but I couldn't wait to get started. I knew I had to monitor my energy and my strength and spend them carefully. I tried to calm down and not get too excited at the beginning of the journey. It was a long way to my goal, the Mason and Dixon Line. Mama and Gram had given me hand-drawn maps and instructions about which routes to take through the woods and what places I absolutely had to avoid. They knew which farms and safe houses were friendly to the Underground Railroad and which plantations I was to circumvent.

Gram gave me specific instructions about where I was to meet up with Moses, who would take the baby from me. There was a creek just over the Mason and Dixon Line, and a special tree beside a creek would be our meeting place. The tree was a triple tree … three trees growing out of one tree trunk. It had been there for a very long time. Gram carefully drew the path I was to follow to reach the creek. This path was not marked on any regular maps. Gram put an "X" at triple tree, the spot where I was to wait for Moses and hand over the baby.

Gram didn't really want to write down anything, in case I was captured, but there wasn't time for me to memorize it all. I could tell that Gram was counting on my memory to get it right, to find the creek and the important triple tree meeting place. The plans had not been as carefully thought through as my mother would have liked. She was a conscientious person and didn't want to get into anything that would put me at risk. But time was critical with this particular mission. I know my mother was having an exceedingly difficult time sending me off on my own again.

We were all worried about this trip for many reasons. One cause for concern was the absence of a clear plan to return me to my home. I would walk for almost two days to get to the Maryland-Delaware line, and I would be exhausted when I'd reached my goal. I would need to rest, and then I would somehow have to get home again to Elderberry Farm. Word had been sent that I would be given a place to rest and a guide with a wagon who would be sure I made it safely back to Burley.

Gram liked to verify every communication that was sent to us, but sometimes that wasn't possible. This was one of those times. She could not verify that I would have a place to rest after I handed over the baby to the next conductor, Moses. Gram was not able to verify that I would have a guide to bring me home. Time was short, and this mission could not be delayed. Everybody decided to go along without the usual confirmations.

I said goodbye to my mother and to Gram. Mama didn't very often cry, but she cried when she said goodbye to me this night. I would take my rowing boat across Crooked Creek to the widow's house, and Grandpa Doc would meet me there with the baby. He would be sure I had everything I needed, to care for this tiny three-day-old child on the journey, and he would walk the first few miles with me. We wanted to do everything we could to be sure the baby didn't cry. Any noise at all might give us away.

I had containers full of goat's milk in the pack on my back. I would carry the baby in a sling across my chest. It was a good deal of extra weight, between the pack and the baby, but I was strong and thought I could manage. The baby was healthy but weighed only six pounds. I stepped into my rowing boat and waved goodbye to my mother and my Gram. We all expected to see each other again in a few days. My mother had tears streaming down her face.

When I reached the widow's farm on the other side of the creek, Grandpa Doc helped me pull my rowing boat up onto the shore. He dragged it into some bushes to hide it. He would take my little boat back across Crooked Creek to Burley after he had launched me on my journey. He told me everything he thought I would need to know about the baby, and he secured the tiny infant in the sling across my chest. The baby was warm against my body, and at this early stage of our trip, she felt light as a feather.

We set off through the woods. My grandfather only occasionally spoke to me, and he always spoke in a whisper. Finally, we reached the point where he had to tell me goodbye. He held me tightly and said he would pray for us to have a safe journey. I saw tears in his eyes as I turned and began my solitary walk. I was determined to be brave because I wanted to be sure this baby grew up as a free human being. I was on my way.

The first part of the trip, even in the dark and through the forest, didn't seem too onerous. I'd traversed several miles and quite a few farm fields, and I made it to a wooded area as dawn was breaking. I'd been told to hide and rest for a while after the sun came up, even if I didn't feel like it. I was energized and didn't want to stop, but I followed the instructions of the people who had done this before me. I removed the pack from my back and fed the baby. We lay down on a bed of pine needles to get some rest, and I put my head down on my pack to use it as a pillow. The baby had not cried at all.

I woke up when the baby began to cry. I changed her diaper and fed her again with the baby-feeding bottle invention my Grandpa Doc had made. After being fed, the baby seemed satisfied and went back to sleep. I drank some water I'd brought, put the pack on my back, and settled the sling that held the baby in front of me. I was ready to continue my journey to freedom.

I walked until I was hungry and the baby was hungry. I ate some of my sandwiches and stopped only to feed the little one. It seemed to me that babies needed to eat much too frequently. Grandpa Doc had warned me about this. He said to feed her whenever she cried. The most important thing was to keep the baby from making any kind of noise which would give us both away. I was ready to rest when darkness came again, but I had the best opportunity to make good time on my journey after sunset. I couldn't rest yet.

The air grew much colder after the sun went down. I

hoped I could keep myself and the baby warm enough. I thought I'd made good progress, but I was worried because I wasn't able to recognize any landmarks that would let me know I was close to Bishopville, Maryland. I knew those who worked for the Underground Railroad used the North Star for guidance. But the sky was dark tonight, and I could not see any stars. When I made it to Bishopville, I would be almost at the Mason and Dixon Line, almost to my goal and journey's end.

I had been told that Moses would find me when I got to the triple tree beside the creek in Sandy Branch, Delaware. She would take the baby from me there. Moses would not cross the line from Delaware into Maryland. I respected that. I just hoped I was going in the right direction and hadn't strayed from the path that had been laid out for me.

I was tired, and I was cold. Feeding the baby and keeping her quiet had slowed me down more than I'd expected. The trip was taking longer than it had been intended to take. I found a stand of trees and decided to get some sleep. It was dark, and I'd eaten all of my sandwiches and finished drinking all of my water. I should be in Bishopville by now. I was worried I might have lost my direction, but I was now too exhausted and frozen to care. I fed the baby and pulled her close to me. We slept soundly in the open air.

When I woke up, it was still dark. Both the baby and I were covered with snow. It wasn't unusual to have snow flurries in late October, but it was rare to have a hard snow fall. My throat was sore, and I wasn't sure I could lift my pack to put it on my back again to continue the journey. I knew I was getting sick with a cold or some other illness, but I had a mission to accomplish. I didn't have the time or the luxury to allow myself to be sick. It was hard going now. The snow was piling up deeper and deeper, the farther north I traveled. I stopped frequently to feed the baby, but I was growing short of goat's milk.

I thought I finally saw the lights of Bishopville, Maryland. I wasn't sure that was where I was, but where else could I be? I knew Sandy Branch was not very far from Bishopville. Sandy Branch was just across that critical line; it was in Delaware. I knew I wasn't at my best, but I made myself stumble on.

As I staggered forward in the blinding snow, I couldn't see where I was going. I tripped as I stepped into a depression in the snow. I tried to untangle my feet so I wouldn't fall, but something grabbed at my ankle. Suddenly, I was on my knees on the ground. I experienced excruciatingly pain and realized immediately what had happened. I had stepped into an animal trap. It was a leg-hold trap. The sharp teeth of the claw bit into my flesh. I was caught and couldn't get loose. The iron clamp around my ankle was tight and heavy and digging into my skin. The trap, intended to catch a small animal, a rabbit or a squirrel, was not intended to ensnare the foot of a human being. I scolded myself for not being more careful, for not watching where my feet were going. The trap had been covered with wet leaves, and the wet leaves had been covered by the falling snow. There was no way I could have seen this menace on the ground in the dark.

I knew something about animal traps. I knew I would not be able to free my leg from its sharp jaws. I also knew that this kind of trap was fastened with a chain to something and was secured in a way that made it impossible for an animal to pull free. I thought I might be able to free myself by finding the other end of the chain that held the trap. If I could manage to separate the chain from whatever held it, I would be able to keep moving forward. I would have to drag the trap and part of the chain along with me, still clinging to my ankle and slowing me down.

I had managed to hold on to the baby when I'd fallen to the ground. I found a log nearby and swept the snow away from it so I could lay the baby down beside me. Thankfully, she stayed asleep. The chain attached to the trap was buried in the dirt. I worked hard, digging with both my hands to free the chain from the frozen ground. My hands and fingers were already numb, but I abandoned my gloves in order to more efficiently pull the dirt away. Finally, I freed the chain. It was old and rusted and heavy. I crawled along the ground and followed the chain to a tree stump where it was securely fastened into the wood. No small animal would be able to pull this trap lose from its moorings.

I knew freeing myself would be difficult, and I had already pushed myself beyond the limits of my endurance. But my situation was critical, and I could not quit.

My mother had made sure to put a sizeable hunting knife into my pack. I searched the pack to find the knife. Then the hard work began. I used the knife to dig away at the wood in the tree stump. It seemed to take forever, and my hands were numb with the cold. Each jab with the knife removed but a tiny bit of wood from around the hardware that secured the chain to the wood. I was known for my persistence in other things, and I was determined that I would not die chained to a tree stump with an animal trap around my ankle. I pulled on the chain and chipped away. Then I pulled some more. Finally, the splintered wood of the stump gave up the rusted U-bolt that had held the chain in place. I fell against the wooden tree trunk with relief, to rest for a few minutes.

I had freed myself from the tree stump, even though I was still held captive by the fanged teeth of the trap and the chain that remained attached to it. The links of the chain were badly rusted. This trap had been abandoned in the woods long ago. If I could find the strength, I thought I might be able to break the chain away from the iron anklet that encircled my foot. If I could free myself of the troublesome chain, I might be able to continue my journey.

I searched for a rock or a length of wood that would allow me to break the rusted links of the chain. I couldn't find anything suitable that I thought might work, so I decided to use the hunting knife again. I sawed back and forth and back and forth with the knife. It was a painful process, and my fingers were almost paralyzed with the cold. I couldn't feel them anymore. Finally, the rusted link I'd been working on broke in two. The chain fell away. I still had the iron claw around my ankle, but the heavy chain was gone.

I picked up the baby and secured her against my chest. I tried to stand, but my legs were weak. I had to grab hold of the tree stump to right myself. The weight around my ankle was still a drag on me as I struggled to make progress through the snow. I could see the prongs of the trap; the spikes were painful and had cut deeply into my skin. I was bleeding and knew I was leaving a trail of blood behind me in the snow. I was in another world as I tried to dissociate myself from the pain and the cold. I was lost.

I knew I was in trouble, but I pushed forward. I wondered if I ought to stop and wait for help, but I decided no help was coming. I stumbled on my way. The wind swirled around me, and I was not able to see where I was going. All of a sudden, the weight around my ankle tripped me up. I'd not been paying attention, and I slipped and fell. I slid into a deep ditch full of water. I was desperate to save the baby, to make sure she didn't get wet. But it was impossible to keep her from falling with me, and she did get wet. Her bunting was soaked, and I knew this could mean the baby might get too cold and freeze to death. I had to find help or someplace dry. I pulled myself out of the ditch. It was so cold outside, and both the baby and I were soaking wet. I was afraid the baby would not survive. I was almost certain that I would not survive.

I was moving slowly now, and I was beyond my limit with exhaustion. I experienced a burst of energy when I discovered an old shed. I decided to leave the baby in the shed. If I could cover the baby with enough pine needles and all of the blankets in my pack, she might live until I could bring help or send someone to rescue her. I would continue on by myself to try to get to the triple tree meeting place in Sandy Branch. I was not thinking clearly at this point. My throat was throbbing, and I ached all over. I was feverish.

After I'd left the baby in the shed, I wandered aimlessly. I stumbled around in the woods, probably going in circles. I focused all of my little remaining energy on trying to remember exactly where in the woods the path had turned off to reach the creek and the triple tree. The snow was blinding, and I couldn't see the ground as I put one foot in front of the other. I guess it was inevitable that sooner or later, I would fall. Sure enough, I slipped on a patch of ice and tumbled down a hillock. The trap around my ankle clanked against the stones as I careened toward the bottom of the slope. I was falling down the bank, into a rushing stream. Before the precipitation had turned to snow, it had been rain in this area. The stream was full, and the water was foaming and angry as it swirled with the wind. I could not stop myself before I rolled into the water.

I was a good swimmer, but I was weighted down, not only by the animal claw, but also with heavy winter clothes and boots and with my pack. Soaked with creek water, the clothes dragged me down deeper and deeper into the churning, freezing maelstrom. I shed the pack from my back and struggled to keep my head above the water's surface. I knew I had to get rid of the heavy clothing that was keeping me from being able to swim to the shore. I could not survive for long in the icy water. As I gathered all my strength and tried desperately to make it to the land, I got caught in an eddy that pulled me away from the shore and into the middle of the stream. As hard as I'd fought to try to find my way out of the water, I now knew that I was going to die.

CHAPTER FIFTEEN

Moses and the Baby

13-15-19-5-19 1-14-4 20-8-5 2-1-2-25

I remember saying my prayers and asking God to take care of the people I loved, my family back in Burley. I asked God to please help Cranky not miss me too much. I prayed that someone would find the baby I had given my all to rescue and that she would be allowed to live. I had tried my hardest, but it had not been enough. I was resigned that I was at the end of my life. My mind was in another place. I went under for the last time.

I thought I had died when I saw an angel in the water beside me. The angel had a black face like Solomon's. The angel looked like Solomon, and I was certain, in my mind-altered state, that it was Solomon who had come to save me. I knew that I must be in heaven now. The angel reached out and took my hand. He was very strong. He held on to me and pulled me after him as he swam toward the shore. He dragged me with him through the water and finally lifted me out of the water onto the bank beside the creek. I found myself on the land, where I lay unable to move. I don't remember anything at all about what happened after that.

I only know what others later told me about how Moses and her friend had found me. I never was able to discover who my guardian angel had been, the person I'd believed was Solomon who had dragged me out of the creek and saved my life. I'd not had any idea where I was at the time. I had become disoriented and lost my bearings in the snow. Wandering from place to place, I'd desperately searched for the place where I was to meet Moses, for the right creek and the right tree. In spite of believing that I had failed to find the right location, in fact, I had fallen into a creek quite near the triple tree, the designated meeting place. It seemed I had fortuitously but unknowingly crossed the Mason and Dixon Line.

Luckily, the shed where I'd left the baby under a pile of pine needles and wet blankets was also in Delaware. Someone, who knew Moses was expecting me and the baby, had come looking for me. She found me lying frozen and unconscious on the bank of the stream close to the triple tree and brought Moses to the site. Moses and her friend were happy to find me, but they were understandably upset not to find the baby with me. Moses and her helper knew that the baby's mother had died, but they'd not been anticipating that anyone as young as I was would be the one to bring the baby to them.

I was able to tell Moses and her helper, through my delirium, that I had left the baby in a shed. They somehow knew where that shed was, and they rescued the baby. When they found her, the baby was screaming with hunger. She was barely warm enough, but she was fine and healthy. Moses saved the life of the baby girl who had been my responsibility, and she sent the little one on her way to freedom in New York State, accompanied by a wet nurse. Saving me would be more difficult.

Moses knew I was in bad shape when she and her friend found me beside the creek. There were just the two of them, and they'd only come to pick up the baby to take her on north, out of Delaware. They'd had no idea who would be bringing the baby, and they were not prepared to take care of a deathly ill young girl. There had been no plan, either to find a place for me to rest or to provide anyone to take me back to Elderberry Farm. Moses could have left me to die, but she had a good heart and great courage. She didn't abandon me to the wolves and the snow. Even though she didn't know my name or exactly where I'd come from, she risked her own capture to save me.

I was a mystery to her, and I was too ill to speak for myself. She knew the first thing she had to do was to move me to someplace warm, out of the snow and damp. She had once known the area around Sandy Branch very well, but recently and for several years, she had lived in Albany, New York. She no longer knew many people in Southern Delaware, and there were even fewer she felt she could trust. Because she had a reputation as a person who smuggled slaves to freedom and was personally such a prize for slave hunters, she tried to keep her movements as secretive as possible. She moved quietly and quickly, without any fuss and without allowing herself to be recognized. She took a chance and contacted a person who was a conductor on the Underground Railroad in Sandy Branch. Luckily for me, that conductor called on a doctor in the town. Dr. Wright was a friend to those who worked the Underground Railroad, so they knew he was a trusted ally who would help me.

I'd been lying on the ground, freezing and covered with snow for hours. I was suffering from extreme cold. I was unconscious and close to death when the doctor and his handyman, another friend of freedom, came to the woods to rescue me from the elements. Moses did not want to be seen anywhere, and she didn't want anybody to see her with me. She was concerned about me, but she had to remain in the shadows. The doctor had no idea who I was or where I had come from. He had only been told that someone needed help and where to find me. They put me on a horse and transported me to the doctor's house. I was unable to tell Dr. Wright that my own dear Grandpa Doc was probably someone he knew.

Doctor Wright and his wife put me in a warm bath to try to bring my body temperature back to normal. They fed me warm chicken broth through a tube … attempting to warm me from the inside and the outside at the same time. They gave me warm sugar water and tried to make me drink it. They wrapped me in blankets and laid me on a cot in front of their kitchen fire. They took turns, and one or the other of them stayed awake all night long, keeping the fire going and watching over me. By morning my body temperature had risen. I was not going to freeze to death, but I was gravely ill. I was unable to speak, and nobody had yet been able to find out who I was.

Dr. Wright and his handyman knew they had to remove the animal trap that was still clamped onto my leg. Dr. Wright later told me about how he and his handyman had removed the jaws of the animal trap from my ankle. It had taken hours of sawing and using a metal rasp to break through the iron.

Dr. Wright was concerned about the wounds he found after the trap was removed. My ankle had quite a few deep tears and cuts that required the doctor to sew the skin back together in several places. His greater concern was that my wounds would become infected. If the blood supply had been cut off to my foot for an extended length of time, gangrene would set in. Dr. Wright might have to amputate. I could lose my foot and even some of my leg.

I later learned that Grandpa Doc and my friend Ollie had ridden their horses all the way to Sandy Branch in the snow to try to find me. My mother and Gram were frantic with worry when the unexpected early snow storm hit the Eastern Shore. Because Moses had been the one to bring me to the attention of the Sandy Branch doctor, the Wrights knew I had been on a mission for the Underground Railroad. They didn't know if slave hunters were looking for me. They were trying to keep it a secret that I was at their house. Grandpa Doc and Ollie searched everywhere but couldn't find me.

Moses heard that Grandpa Doc was looking for his granddaughter Louisa Gates, and somehow she got word to him that I was with the Sandy Branch doctor. At last, Dr. Wright and his wife knew who I was, and they warmly welcomed Dr. Edward Preston Taylor when he came to see about me. They offered Grandpa Doc and Ollie a room in their house and fed them while the doctors consulted over my medical condition.

Both physicians agreed that I was suffering from a critical case of pneumonia. I had a high fever, and when they listened with a stethoscope, they realized that both of my lungs were full of fluid. It was difficult for me to breathe. I was so gravely ill with the pneumonia that I could die. Many people die who contract this disease of the lungs. Grandpa Doc sent Ollie back to Burley to let my mother and my Gram know that I'd been found. Ollie also had to take them the disturbing news that I was terribly ill, could not be moved, and might not survive. It would be two weeks before the doctors were certain I would live. It would be another week still before Dr. Wright was certain that the wounds on my ankle would heal. There was no gangrene, and I would not lose my foot.

Grandpa Doc and Doctor Wright decided it would be wise not to let anybody know that I was in Sandy Branch and recovering at the Wright's house. Grandpa Doc had patients in Burley that needed his attention, and Doctor Wright convinced him to return home. My mother wanted to immediately travel to the Wright's house to take care of me. But because of the mission I'd just completed and my association with the Underground Railroad, my family decided it would be best if my mother and Gram stayed in Burley and pretended that I was sick at home, in my own bed at the farm.

When I missed school, my teachers, my classmates, and everyone in town would wonder what had happened to me. It would not be a good idea for anybody to know that I had become ill while smuggling a slave's newborn daughter out of Maryland and into Delaware. It was safer for all concerned to believe that I had never been to Delaware and that I had come down with pneumonia in my own house, in my own home state. My mother agreed to go along with this ruse, but I was told later that she was frantic to come to Delaware to care for me.

CHAPTER SIXTEEN

The King of Israel Has Reached the Promised Land

20-8-5   11-9-14-7   15-6   9-19-18-1-5-12   8-1-19   18-5-1-3-8-5-4
20-8-5   16-18-15-13-9-19-5-4   12-1-14-4

hile I was struggling to survive at the doctor's house in Sandy Branch, Moses came to visit me. She sat by my bed one whole night and held my hand. But I don't remember any of that. I don't remember ever laying eyes on Moses, but the Wrights told me later that she had indeed been to their house to see me.

I do remember that I constantly had dreams and terrible nightmares, as I lay on my cot, trying to stay alive. I dreamed of Cranky and Ithaca. I dreamed about Joseph and my mother. I dreamed of the father I had never met but whose portrait hung over the fireplace mantle in our front parlor at Elderberry Farm. I dreamed of Solomon and of Becky Sharpe. I was delirious and hallucinating from the high fevers and chills brought on by the disease that wracked my body.

I had vivid dreams of Ava, the girl who lived on the plantation next to Elderberry Farm. In my nightmares, her perfect hair, that was always neatly secured in braids with ribbons that matched her dresses, had come undone from her pigtails and was streaming out behind her, flying in the wind like the locks of a banshee. She had lost her ribbons, and her eyes were wild with madness. She had her arms raised and ran towards me in an aggressive and threatening manner. I always woke up just before Ava reached me. I later wondered what would have happened to me, if I hadn't awakened just in time.

I clearly remember one dream, or maybe it was not a dream, of Moses whispering in my ear. She spoke softly in a voice I could scarcely understand. "The King of Israel is alive and well and free! The King of Israel has reached the Promised Land." She murmured it three times in my ear. I later interpreted this to mean that Solomon had reached Philadelphia and was doing fine. But I didn't know if I had dreamed this, if it was wishful thinking, or if it had really happened.

Moses said other things to me, or maybe I dreamed those as well. She told me that "my friend was praying for my recovery." She told me that "my friend was doing very well in school in Philadelphia." She told me I was the youngest conductor ever on the Underground Railroad, and she was proud of me. She said she would never forget the name Louisa Taylor Gates. She said the baby I had saved was her grandniece, and I had given her, Moses, a special gift when I had carried the infant to freedom. She said the family had decided to name the baby Louisa, after me. I imagined I'd heard all of these things when I was in a feverish state, so I have no idea if I'd really heard them or if any of them were true.

My fever finally broke, and it appeared that I was going to live. Because I'd been young and healthy before I became ill, I was able to survive the pneumonia. I was one of the lucky ones. Many people, who had been as sick as I had been, died after being struck down by pneumonia. The Wrights had taken good care of me, and it was because of their good care and constant attention to me in my debilitated state, that I had survived. I owed them a great debt.

When I was well enough to travel, Grandpa Doc came to Sandy Branch with a wagon to carry me home to Burley. It was a crisp November day, and the sun was shining. A mattress had been placed in the bed of the wagon, and the Wrights helped me walk outside and lifted me into the wagon. I was so weak, I was not able to walk without help, let alone climb up into a wagon by myself. I waved goodbye to my new Delaware friends. I think they were sad to see me go. I was a little bit sad to leave them, too, but I couldn't wait to see Mama, Gram, and Cranky. With many blankets and quilts piled on top of me to keep me warm, I lay on the mattress in the back of the wagon and slept most of the way home. It seemed like it was a terribly bumpy ride and took a long time to get to Elderberry Farm. I wondered if I would ever be myself again, if I would ever have my strength and stamina back.

My mother ran to the wagon to greet me. The last time I had seen her, weeks earlier, she'd had tears streaming down her face. Today, she again had tears, but these were tears of joy. I was so worn out from the journey, I could only squeeze her hand. Sally and Grandpa Doc lifted me out of the wagon and carried me into the parlor. My mother had set up a bed for me there in front of the fireplace. I would not have to climb the stairs to get to my bedroom. My mother fussed, bringing water to put beside my bed and asking if I wanted something to eat. It was all I could do to give her a weak smile. I could see she wanted more of a response from me, but that was all I had to give her at the moment.

Just as I was drifting off to sleep again, the door to the parlor opened, and Cranky, my beloved little white dog, ran into the room. She jumped up on the bed and licked and licked my face. I was so happy to see her. I grabbed hold of her and pulled her under the blankets with me. Being close to Cranky would keep me company and help me recover. The next few days and weeks ran together in my mind as I tried to eat healthy food and struggled to walk and regain the strength in my legs. I was impatient with my progress. My mother kept reminding me that I had been deathly ill and that my recovery would be slow.

I worked on being patient, but even Cranky longed for me to hurry up and get better so we could go on walks together like we used to do.

Grandpa Doc came to see me every day. He always acted as if he was pleased with my progress, even when I knew he really wasn't. He told me I was his star patient, but I think he said that just because I was his granddaughter and he loved me so much. My Gram also came every day. She brought me little pots of vanilla egg custard, jars of raspberry jam, and other things that she and Celia had made especially for me and knew I loved.

I told Mama about the dreams I'd had while I was in the midst of the feverish state of my illness. I told her about dreaming that Moses had come to sit by my bed and had whispered news of Solomon in my ear. My mother said she thought that must really have happened, that I hadn't dreamed it. She confirmed that she and Gram and Grandpa Doc had also received news that Solomon had finally made it to Philadelphia and was doing very well in school. When I heard this report from my mother, the news about Solomon that verified what I thought Moses had told me, a weight lifted from my heart, and I began to heal more rapidly.

When I was well enough to resume my school work, my mother brought home lessons from my teacher at the school in Burley. I could not yet go to school and spend all day there. I still had to rest often, and it would have been impossible for me to walk the two miles or even ride my pony to town from Elderberry Farm. School work had always been easy for me, so I didn't have any trouble catching up with what I'd missed while I'd been sick. When I'd regained some of my energy, I would go to stay with Gram and Grandpa Doc at their house in town so I could walk across the street to attend school. I loved school and would be happy to go back when I was able.

Some important things had happened in the world since I'd traveled with the newborn baby to Sandy Branch. On November 6th, my grandfather had cast his vote for Abraham Lincoln to be President of the United States. My mother and my grandmother are outraged that women still can't vote in the United States of America. Gram says that once slavery is abolished, her next project is going to be to get the laws changed in this country so that women are allowed to vote.

The 1860 election was an important one for my family and for the entire country. We all felt strongly that Mr. Lincoln was the best candidate. Lincoln belongs to the Republican Party, the anti-slavery party. Another candidate running for President was John Breckenridge who had formed a new political party, the Southern Democrats. The Southern Democrats are different from the Northern Democrats and have a different political agenda. Breckenridge and his party are more in favor of allowing slavery to continue to exist in the United States than any of the other candidates or political parties. We absolutely did not want him to win the election, but all the slave owners in our part of Maryland had campaigned and voted for him.

My Gram likes to point out that Negroes, people of African heritage who have dark skin, who are free, can vote in Massachusetts and in several other northern states. There are quite a few free Negroes in Massachusetts and throughout New England, and many of them own land and businesses. These free black men are allowed to vote in all elections, including for President of the United States.

It would take a long time for all the ballots to be counted, and we wouldn't know for some time who'd won the election. The President is actually chosen by the Electoral College. All the votes from all the states have to be counted, and then the Electoral College will cast its ballots. We have our fingers crossed that Mr. Lincoln will be the next President of the United States. The new President will take the oath of office on March 4, 1861. We prayed every night that the United States would not suffer a schism, but everyone fears that civil war is a real possibility.

CHAPTER SEVENTEEN

Joy to the World

10-15-15   20-15   20-8-5   23-15-18-12-4

I t had taken many weeks, but by the time the Christmas season approached, I was almost fully recovered from my near-fatal illness. Joseph is scheduled to come home from Washington, D.C. to celebrate Christmas and the New Year with us. I have to admit I will be glad to see him. My mother's sister Margaret and her husband Angus will be bringing Joseph to Burley, and my cousins Lane and Richard will also make the trip. I have the best cousins. Lane is two years older than I am, and she is exceptionally smart and also very beautiful. Richard is younger, but he's a lot of fun and smart, too. Margaret and Angus have a fancy covered carriage and two prize-winning black horses that they will drive down to Burley for the Christmas holidays. Their carriage can carry six people, and with two horses and special wheels, it can travel on our snow-covered dirt roads. My relatives are city people now, but my Aunt Margaret grew up in Burley.

We are planning to have a party at Elderberry Farm while my cousins are visiting. We will invite all the neighbors and have roast goose, warm spiced apple cider, a country ham with biscuits and elderberry jam, and all kinds of special Christmas cakes and cookies. We will have music at our party. Two friends of our family will play the fiddle. My Aunt Margaret will also play the fiddle with the group. She is quite accomplished and calls her fiddle a violin. Another woman and Mama will play their recorders. My mother has been playing the recorder since she was a little girl, and she can play anything. People will dance. Some of the neighbors won't come because they don't agree with our family's views about slavery, and they don't like our family. We won't miss those died-in-the-wool slave owners anyway. The people we really like will want to come to our party.

My favorite thing about Christmas is going out into the woods and chopping down our own Christmas tree. We have a high ceiling in our front hall, and there is room there for a very tall tree. We save most of our tree decorations from year to year, but we string fresh strands of cranberries and popcorn every Christmas. My mother makes beautiful tree ornaments out of the seashells she collects from the Assateague Island beach. She paints them with colorful designs and puts a tiny hole in each one. She puts a string through the hole, and we use this string to hang the ornament on the tree. We collect pine cones and paint them bright colors. Pine cones make quite agreeable tree decorations, and they don't cost anything, except for the paint. Some people put candles on their Christmas trees, but my family doesn't think it is safe to have fire around our tree.

Every year, Gram orders Christmas gifts from Boston and New York for all of us. She buys books and toys and candy for her grandchildren. She buys big jars of Vermont maple syrup for Grandpa Doc. She has silk dresses made for her daughters. She usually buys everyone a new winter coat. Since the railroad tracks now go all the way from Philadelphia to Seaford and to Sandy Branch, it doesn't take nearly as long as it used to for Gram's packages to arrive from the big cities on the East Coast. My Gram opens up her heart and her pocketbook for Christmas.

It's a tradition that our family celebrates Christmas Eve with a turkey dinner at Elderberry Farm. We always have oyster stew and oysters prepared in other ways. One of our favorite ways to eat oysters is called "Oysters Fitzpatrick." We have delicious oysters in Burley in December. We get them from Chincoteague, Virginia which is just a few miles down the road. My mother, Aunt Margaret, and Gram make two kinds of stuffing to go with the turkey. They make plain bread stuffing with onions, celery, parsley, thyme, and sage for the Yankees. This is the kind of stuffing my Gram learned to make and always ate when she was growing up in Boston. Because we are in the South, we also make southern cornbread stuffing that has sausage and onions and other herbs and seasonings in it. Both are delicious, and I can't ever decide which one I want to eat first. We have cranberry relish, sweet potato biscuits, and for dessert, there are pumpkin and pecan pies. I always think, after I have stuffed myself with turkey and pecan pie, that I will not be able to eat anything more for weeks. But by the next day, I somehow am ready to eat again.

After dinner, we go to church for Christmas Eve midnight services and sing all the Christmas carols. I love to sing, and it is especially fun to sing with my family lined up in one church pew. We all have good, loud voices. At the end of the service, we each light a small candle during the singing of *Silent Night*. We carry these lighted candles outside into the December darkness as we exit the church.

When we get home from church, we hang our stockings on the mantle in the parlor at Elderberry Farm. Not many people in Burley hang stockings on the mantle as part of their Christmas traditions. Gram brought this wonderful custom with her from Boston. I know, even before morning comes, that I will have a big beautiful orange in the toe of my stocking. Oranges are hard to find in December, and they are costly. But my mother always makes sure everybody in our family has an orange. There are special candies of all kinds and other small gifts in my stocking. On Christmas morning, we unwrap the gifts that are under our tree before we put on dress-up clothes and climb in the carriage to go to town.

We go to Gram and Grandpa Doc's house in Burley for dinner on Christmas Day. We celebrate another whole Christmas there before we sit down to dinner. Gram loves Christmas, and she has her house decorated with garlands of greens and boxwood everywhere, inside and outside. There are holly wreaths with wide red ribbons and bows on the doors and candles at every window. She works for weeks making the garlands and the wreaths and getting it all arranged just so. It's hard for her now because she has rheumatism in her fingers, but it is important to her to decorate everything for Christmas.

Gram and Grandpa Doc also have a huge Christmas tree. They have collected Christmas ornaments for many years, and my Gram brought some of these with her from New England where she celebrated Christmases as a child. Our grandparents have many gifts under their Christmas tree, and we always look forward to opening their fun presents. We have two Christmas celebrations. After all the gifts have been unwrapped, we sit down to Christmas dinner.

We eat late in the day because Gram wants her hired hands to have time to celebrate Christmas with their families before they have to come to her house to help with our big meal. Celia supervises the cooking, and there are several Negroes who serve the dinner. Gram puts her best linen tablecloths woven in Ireland on the dining room table. She uses matching linen napkins, and the silverware is made of sterling. The glassware sparkles, and Gram's finest Limoges dishes from France fill the long table where we all sit. There are arrangements of magnolia leaves and red wax candles in silver candle-holders in the center of the table. Every year at Christmas time, red and white camellia bushes bloom in our part of Maryland. Gram has a hedge of camellia bushes at the side of her house, and she picks the flowers that morning to put on the table for Christmas Day dinner. The table looks magnificent. Seeing freshly picked red and white flower blossoms on the table in the middle of winter always makes me feel as if I am in a magical place.

Grandpa Doc gives a mini-sermon of sorts before we can begin to eat. He loves to say grace before each meal, and he loves to pray. Sometimes I think he might have preferred to become a preacher rather than a doctor. In his Christmas dinner grace, he talks about the year and what has happened to all of us. He talks about all the good things that have occurred, and he talks about the challenges we have faced. He remembers the people we've loved and cared about who have died during the year. He even mentions special pets and horses that have passed on. It is quite an interesting talk, but sometimes he goes on and on for much too long. Everyone can smell the wonderful aromas coming from the kitchen, and we wonder when Grandpa Doc will sit down and be quiet so we can eat. One year, Gram lost patience, interrupted him, and said, "All right, Doc, that's enough. The lobster bisque is getting cold." Everybody laughed

... even Grandpa Doc. We all know who the real boss is around here.

Gram serves several courses for Christmas dinner. She and Celia have been cooking and preparing for days. Gram orders exotic foods sent from New York and Boston for the dinner. We have lobster bisque for the first course. Then we have shrimp and crabmeat in a special remoulade sauce that my grandmother learned to make when she went to a cooking school in Louisiana. She learned to make many wonderful dishes when she was living in New Orleans, before she met and married Grandpa Doc.

The main course is a standing rib roast of beef that has been specially ordered. Celia serves a delicious bread dish called Yorkshire pudding that is made with lots of eggs and accompanies the rib roast. This savory pudding puffs up and rises high in the oven. It is crispy on the outside and creamy like custard on the inside. It is so delicious. We have Yorkshire pudding only at Christmas. I guess it is a lot of trouble to make it come out just right. I love it, and I put butter on my slices and eat it like I would a biscuit or a roll. There is beef gravy and a spicy horseradish with cream sauce to put on the meat. We have roasted potatoes and our own stewed tomatoes with home-churned cheese. Celia always makes green beans with onions and smoked ham. Everybody's favorite is acorn squash that's baked with walnuts, cinnamon, butter, and some of the Vermont maple syrup Gram buys for Grandpa Doc. He loves the acorn squash so much that Grandpa Doc eats at least two halves. I think if it were up to him, he would skip the roast beef and all the rest of it and just eat the squash. He also loves the Yorkshire pudding, like I do.

For dessert, Gram and Celia always make a big plum pudding. Gram pours something with alcohol in it all over the pudding and lights it on fire. When she carries it into the dining room on a silver platter, it looks like a blazing crown. It is a very dramatic presentation. My Gram likes to have some drama in her life. The alcohol burns off, and the fire goes out. The sweet pudding is served in small pieces with a yummy white concoction called "hard sauce." I don't know why they call it hard sauce because it's soft and buttery and sweet. It's not hard at all. The servings of pudding are small because it is such a rich dessert. It just isn't possible to eat a lot of the Christmas plum pudding that's made with beef suet, raisins, dates, currents, and dark molasses. I am usually so full of all the other delicious food by the time Gram arrives with her blazing crown of plum pudding, I can barely eat any.

My Gram is very frugal about many things in her life, but when it comes to food and to Christmas, she throws caution and her budget to the winds. She spends freely and generously to give us all beautiful gifts and wonderful memories. I am so thankful that I was born into this family that has traditions and celebrates holidays with such grand style.

After dinner, we go to Gram and Grandpa Doc's parlor so the grownups can drink coffee and eat after-dinner cheeses and sweets. There are figs and dates, walnuts and pecans, and several kinds of cheese. I especially love the homemade caramel candies dipped in bitter-sweet chocolate. The children play with their toys, and I find a quiet corner where I curl up with a book Gram has given me for Christmas.

This year, she gave me two books, and I had a time deciding which to read first. One of the books is *A Tale of Two Cities*, a new novel by Charles Dickens. The other book is a special edition of *Uncle Tom's Cabin* by Harriet Beecher Stowe. My mother read *Uncle Tom's Cabin* to me a few years ago, but this is my own copy of the book that is a family favorite. I can now read it for myself. I finally decided to begin reading the book by Charles Dickens. It's about the French Revolution and sounds as if it will be quite exciting.

I'd almost drifted off to sleep when Gram tapped me on the shoulder. She was holding a package wrapped in brown paper and string. "This gift arrived for you late last night, on Christmas Eve, while we were all at church. It was left on our front porch, and I don't know who brought it. It's addressed to you. It looks to be a very special Christmas gift."

I could not imagine who might have sent this package to me. I'd received so many gifts already. Everyone I knew had already given me a wonderful and generous Christmas present. I pulled off the string and carefully opened the brown paper. Inside was a small, perfectly folded, and beautifully colored quilt. It was the size one might put over a baby who was sleeping in a cradle. The pattern was so intricate, and the sewing was so fine, it was hard to imagine that human fingers could have made these tiny quilting stitches. Everyone oohed and aahed over the beauty of the baby quilt.

My mother picked it up and put it to her cheek. She was the one who noticed that there were letters worked subtly into the design of the fabric. She traced the letters, and sure enough, almost hidden in the elaborate design of the quilt were my initials … "L T G" for Louisa Taylor Gates. If you weren't looking for it, you might never see the letters that were cleverly and covertly obscured in the pattern. The quilt was so lovely and so special, I began to cry. Where had this work of art come from? Who had made this wonderful keepsake especially for me?

We had all been so overwhelmed with the beauty of the quilt, and we'd almost missed the two small envelopes that had also been wrapped inside the brown paper package. One note read:

Dear Louisa,
Someday you will have a baby of your own. When you hold that beloved child in your arms, always remember the infant whose life you saved when you carried her to freedom. We are forever grateful.

Very truly yours,
Your Friends in the Lord

The quilt and the note had to be from Moses. Hardly anybody else knew about the newborn I had smuggled across the Mason and Dixon Line a few weeks earlier.

"The quilt has to be from Moses. But I don't know who could have written the note. Moses is brilliant at what she does, but I don't think anyone has ever taught her to read and write. This is quite an eloquent note, and although I have no doubt that these could be her words, I don't think she would have been able to write them down."

"Open the other note. Maybe that one will tell you more." Mama was as curious as I was about who had written to me.

I opened the second envelope, and there were two closely-written pages inside. When I saw the first word, I knew who had composed this letter. I would have recognized Solomon's writing anywhere. Since I was the one who had taught him to write, I ought to recognize his penmanship. I read his letter aloud to everyone. It was full of his wonder at finally being free, his new family whom he adored, his success at his excellent school, and his hopes for the future. He said he could not let us know his new name or where he was living. That had to remain a secret for now. He said he hoped one day I would be able to write back and give him the news of Elderberry Farm, Burley, myself, and my family. His letter sounded so happy. I read the letter a second time. He signed it "with love to all from The King of Israel." It had been an extraordinary year for me, topped off by an extra special Christmas.

CHAPTER EIGHTEEN

Let My People Go

12-5-20   13-25   16-5-15-16-12-5   7-15

e knew before Christmas that Abraham Lincoln had won the election. When he was inaugurated in March of 1861, he would be the new President of the United States. He'd been my family's favorite, so we were all delighted with the results of the voting. But many people in Maryland and throughout the South were not happy about having Lincoln as their President. They had wanted the Southern Democrat, John Breckenridge, to win. Slave owners believed that Breckenridge would be more tolerant of slavery in the states where it already existed and in the new states that would become a part of the United States in the years to come. Slave owners did not

like Abraham Lincoln, and there was much talk about secession and forming a new country made up of states that wanted a guarantee that slavery would continue to be legal. South Carolina seceded from the nation on December 20, 1860, just five days before Christmas.

Those of us who wanted slavery to be outlawed in the United States had high hopes that President Lincoln would do the right thing and ban slavery. The men in my family who were old enough to vote had voted for him because they believed he was a moral man whose heart would lead him to free the slaves. My mother and her parents trusted that Lincoln believed slavery was wrong, and they had faith that eventually he would have the courage and the political will to put an end to it.

Newspapers were full of the controversy. Voices spoke out passionately on both sides of the issue. Tensions were high all over the country, and tensions were high in Maryland and in Burley. People in our small town felt strongly and were deeply divided. Ours was a state in which slavery was still allowed by law, but many wanted Maryland to join other slave states who were talking about secession. Some even talked of civil war. It was a frightening time.

During the Christmas holidays, we'd put aside politics and talk of a divided nation, but when the new year of 1861 arrived, no one anywhere in the United States could avoid acknowledging the trouble that was on the horizon.

The nation was torn over the issues of slavery and states' rights. The signs of trouble had been obvious for a long time to anyone who'd cared to see them. The depth of the fracture was felt in my home town of Burley as well as throughout the entire nation. Abraham Lincoln's election as President sadly served as the catalyst for the secession movement and ultimately for civil war.

The states of Alabama, Florida, Georgia, Louisiana, Mississippi, and Texas followed South Carolina's lead and seceded in February 1861 when the slave-holding states convened a constitutional convention that established the Confederacy. Abraham Lincoln had not even been sworn in as President of the United States, and already seven southern states had separated and formed their own country.

During the late winter and early spring of 1861, things went from bad to worse. On April 12, 1861, just a little over a month after Abraham Lincoln officially became the leader of what remained of our nation, the first shots of the Civil War were fired at Fort Sumter in South Carolina. After these shots were fired, the states of Virginia, North Carolina, Tennessee, and Arkansas also seceded from the Union and joined the Confederacy. Eleven states had formed their own country, the Confederate States of America, and were taking up arms against the United States of America. Hearing that my country was at war with itself was the worst news of my life. The states were plunged into a terrible and divisive conflict, and I realized this war would bring an end to my childhood. Life on Elderberry Farm, life in Burley, and life in the United States would be changed forever.

Union troops poured into Maryland. Battles were fought. Ava was sent away from her plantation house near Burley to live with relatives in Alabama. As strong defenders of slavery, her family stood staunchly with the Confederacy. They were more in sympathy with the people of Alabama than they were with those of us who lived in the border state of Maryland. At least we didn't have to worry about Ava spying on us anymore.

We were strong, and even as a war raged around us, we continued to move slaves out of bondage to freedom. We continued to hang our quilts on the line and to conduct passengers along the diverse and complicated routes of the Underground Railroad. We worked for the day when there would be an end to slavery, a time when no man, woman, or child was legally anyone's possession to be bought and sold. We dreamed of a day when everyone who lived in the United States was free. We longed for a time when the quilt code would no longer be needed, when the Underground Railroad would be just a footnote in history, and when no human being had dominion over another.

Epilogue

5-16-9-12-15-7-21-5

On January 1, 1863, President Abraham Lincoln issued The Emancipation Proclamation. The Emancipation Proclamation freed all the slaves who were being held in bondage in the Confederacy, the southern states which had seceded and were fighting against Union forces in the Civil War.

The Thirteenth Amendment to the Constitution became the law of the land on January 31, 1865. With this legislation, the United States Congress formally and legally abolished slavery in the United States.

Abraham Lincoln was re-elected in 1864. He was inaugurated on March 4, 1865 and began his second term as President of the United States.

The Civil War officially came to an end a few weeks later, on April 9, 1865, when the army of the Confederacy under General Robert E. Lee, surrendered to Union forces at Appomattox Court House, Virginia.

Just five days after the Civil War ended, on April 14, 1865, Abraham Lincoln, 16th President of the United States, was shot in the head by a Confederate sympathizer while attending a play, *Our American Cousin*, at Ford's Theatre in Washington, D.C. Lincoln died the following morning, Saturday, April 15th at 7:22 a.m.

CYPHER KEY

A 1
B 2
C 3
D 4
E 5
F 6
G 7
H 8
I 9
J 10
K 11
L 12
M 13
N 14
O 15
P 16
Q 17
R 18
S 19
T 20
U 21
V 22
W 23
X 24
Y 25
Z 26

AUTHOR'S NOTE:
THE OHIO TUNNELS, A PERSONAL ANECDOTE

When I was a junior in high school, I spent the day with a group of friends at a farm in Southern Ohio. We drove to the remote country farmhouse and were given a tour. Our host's parents told us that the 19th century home on the property had been a stop on the "Underground Railroad." I'd heard adults in my own family, which had Quaker roots, discuss the Underground Railroad. In my American History classes at school, I had read about the complicated and clandestine journeys that those who sought to escape from slavery and gain their freedom had made on the Underground Railroad. But this was the real thing. Slaves had actually made their escapes when they passed through this farm that was not too far from the Ohio River.

We were shown the basement of the farm house. A massive wooden hutch had been pushed aside to reveal a hole in the stone wall of the cellar. We had to duck down to get through the low doorway which led to a maze of complex and confusing tunnels. We spent most of the rest of the day exploring these tunnels. There were dead ends. There were loops that led us back around to where we had started. There were places where the passageways became very narrow, and for several yards, we had to step sideways through the tunnel.

There were only two routes in the intricate and bewildering network that led to the outside ... into the woods and freedom. You would have to know the tunnel exceptionally well to be able to consistently find one of the two ways to exit. If you were not intimately acquainted with the tunnels, you would inevitably make a wrong turn and end up back where you'd begun, or you would find yourself at a dead end. It was a fascinating and sophisticated labyrinth.

I have never forgotten that day and the lessons I learned first-hand by exploring and climbing through the actual tunnels of the Underground Railroad. They were still intact a century after they had been used by escaping slaves. As a free state and on the way to Canada, Ohio was an important waystation on the routes of the Underground Railroad. I have attempted to recreate a sense of the "warren of tunnels hidden behind the hutch in the cellar" in my description of Grandpa Doc and Gram Taylor's basement in Burley, Maryland. I am delighted to be able to share a part of my own personal experience, from my teenage years, in *The Quilt Code*.

AUTHOR'S NOTE:
THE QUILT CONTROVERSY

I am well aware of the controversy about whether or not quilts really were used as a means of sending messages among people who worked to move slaves to freedom along the Underground Railroad. A few well-known historians say the use of quilts to send signals is a myth, folklore, and hearsay, and is not based in documented fact. Other experts argue that most slaves could not read or write. Therefore, any activities in which slaves were engaged would rarely, if ever, be written down. Even if they could read and write, participants would never have recorded what they were doing for fear of retaliation … severe punishment or death.

The key to a covert cypher is, by definition, not written down. Whatever quilt code *might* have been used would have been shrouded in secrecy. Even those who could read and write would not have written down the fact that there was such a code, let alone how to interpret the signals. A quilt code was a means to communicate in secret. It would have been foolhardy and impossible for the use of such a code to have been documented in a way that would have been acceptable to those who rigorously and religiously require the use of footnotes and bibliographies. Because it was covert, it was not the sort of activity that would have been documented. It was not that kind of code.

Any use of a quilt code would have had to have been local and personal. If there had been widespread use of "a code" everyone would have known about it, including those who lived on plantations, slave owners, and slave hunters. There could never have been a national or state-wide code. It would have been impossible and worthless to disseminate a wide-spread code. There would never even have been a quilt code that was used generally in a town or even in a neighborhood. If whatever secrecy was attached to the cypher became widely known, it would instantly become useless as a covert means of communication. Therefore, it follows that the code would have had to be very closely held. Its use would have had to be extremely limited geographically and known to a very small and circumscribed group of people. Each local faction would have developed its own code, shared only by a small circle of those in the know.

The code would have had to be dynamic. It could not have stayed the same, day in and day out, year in and year out. The quilts were publicly displayed, for all to see. If the code never changed, it would have been too easy, even over a short period of time, to crack the code. Therefore, to remain secret, to maintain its covert cypher status, the code had to change on a daily and or weekly basis. The system for these changes would have been known to only a few participants.

My story about how the quilt code *might* have been used is not meant to minimize the horrors of slavery or to ignore the plight of those who were unable to escape from the plantation.

Acknowledgments

The first thank you is to my readers: Jane Rogers Corcoran, Amy Louisa Taylor, Robert Lane Taylor, David Heltzel, Bettyrose Schwier-Hetzel, Lane Taylor Worthing, Peggy Baker, Nancy Calland Hart, and Lenane Turner Figge. Additional and heartfelt thanks go to those who edited the story for me: Nancy Calland Hart, David Hetzel, Bettyrose Schwier-Hetzel, Amy Louisa Taylor, and Robert Lane Taylor. A special shout out of recognition goes to my granddaughter, Lane Taylor Worthing, for her comments and editing skills. All of your excellent suggestions and your sharp eyes are very much appreciated.

I want to give a special thank you to my husband Robert who drove me to both Harriet Tubman museums and pushed my wheelchair around the streets of Cambridge, Maryland and across the parking lots of the Church Creek, Maryland national park exhibit. Without his help, I probably would not have been able to visit these museums. *The Quilt Code* has been greatly enriched with the addition of elements from the Harriet Tubman story.

I am grateful to Jaime Coston who took Louisa's beautiful design and transformed it into a brilliant book cover. I always appreciate the professional and conscientious help from Jamie Tipton of Open Heart Designs who completed the layout of the cover. She designs and formats the interior of the book so that it can be printed and published. She has recently expanded her business, and that has been my good luck. Jamie's expert and creative hands have worked hard to guide my manuscript all the way through to its final book form. Thanks to Andrea Lopez Burns whose excellent photography work always makes me look good.

It is a long process to bring a story from the imagination to the finished product in the form of a completed and tangible novel. I could not have done it without a tremendous amount of help from my team.

The first question Elizabeth Burke, M.D. always asked me when I saw her in her office was: "What's new and exciting in your life?" I promised myself that one day I would have a good answer for her. Thank you, Dr. Burke.

Other books by
Margaret Turner Taylor

SECRET IN THE SAND

BASEBALL DIAMONDS

TRAIN TRAFFIC

www.margaretttaylorwrites.com

CPSIA information can be obtained
at www.ICGtesting.com
Printed in the USA
BVHW051040300620
582404BV00007B/14/J

9 781734 734737